Steve the Sure

Books by Mary Towne

Wanda the Worrywart
Their House
Steve the Sure

Steve the Sure
Mary Towne

Atheneum   1990   New York

Collier Macmillan Canada
TORONTO
Maxwell Macmillan International Publishing Group
NEW YORK   OXFORD   SINGAPORE   SYDNEY

Atheneum
Macmillan Publishing Company
866 Third Avenue
New York, NY 10022

Collier Macmillan Canada, Inc.
1200 Eglinton Avenue East
Suite 200
Don Mills, Ontario M3C 3N1

First Edition
Printed in the United States of America
Designed by Kimberly M. Hauck
1 2 3 4 5 6 7 8 9 10

Towne, Mary
Steve the sure/Mary Towne.—1st ed.
p.   cm.
Summary: While vacationing with his family at a friendly but somewhat
shabby Vermont resort, Steve, who knows he is nearly always right about most
things, decides to find a way to help ease the resort's financial plight.
ISBN 0-689-31646-1
[1. Vacations—Fiction. 2. Hotels, motels, etc.—Fiction.
3. Interpersonal relations—Fiction.] I. Title.
PZ7.T6495Sr 1990
[Fic]—dc20   90-584
                                                  CIP
                                                  AC

Author's Note

Potter's Lodge is loosely based on Quimby Country, a family resort in Vermont's North-east Kingdom. No resemblance is intended between my characters and actual guests or staff members at Quimby's. I have also taken a good many liberties as to details of setting and accommodation.

Steve the Sure

Chapter 1

Steve watched the ball sail by without lifting his racket. "Out," he said, as it took a high sideways hop off the worn beige clay of the tennis court.

"Are you sure?" asked Dr. North from the other side of the net, wiping the sweat from his eyes with a beefy forearm.

"Yep." Steve nodded, and showed him how far out with his hands—three or four inches.

"Oh, well, if Steve is *sure* . . . ," said someone on the sidelines with a laugh.

"Actually, Steve has exceptional eyesight," he heard his aunt Marge say.

"C'mon, Angie." Steve motioned his sister to the other side of the center line and got ready to serve again, this time to Dr. North's daughter Sally. "Fifteen all. No, play *up*, remember? Close to the net."

Angie turned and made a face at him, rolling her large

blue eyes, which were several shades lighter than Steve's own, and also several shades vaguer. "What's the point of playing up if Sally never hits it to me?"

Steve sighed and walked forward. Their opponents weren't ready yet, anyway. Sally was looking for the third ball among the weeds back in the corner, poking around languidly with the handle of her racket, while her father stood watching with his hands on his hips, looking resigned.

"The point is, you can *move*, Angie. She doesn't have to hit the ball straight at you for you to hit it back, not with those soft, dinky little shots she's been making. What you want to do is sneak over and smack it right back at her. We need to make Sally hit the ball more," he explained. "So far her father's been doing all the work."

"Well, but he's getting tired," Angie pointed out hopefully.

"Not tired enough," Steve told her. "Listen, we're behind five games to two, and if we lose this game, we lose the set and we're out of the tournament."

"Oh. I thought it was only four–two. Anyway, are you sure? That we're out, I mean? This whole round-robin deal is so confusing."

Angie looked distractedly over at the chart tacked to the trunk of the tall sugar maple that shaded the strip of lawn where spectators sat or sprawled—mostly other players waiting their turn. "Potter's Mixed Doubles #57," the chart was grandly headed, meaning this was the fifty-seventh year the tournament had been held at Potter's Lodge and Family Camp. All guests over the age of six were welcome to participate, each team to play one set against every other team, time and weather permitting, the four winning teams to meet on the weekend for semifinals and finals.

In theory, no one was ever actually out of the tournament; but in practice, time and weather took their toll, and losing teams tended to wander off in search of something better to do once arithmetic proved they had no chance of making the final four. That was what Steve meant by "out." Certainly he himself had no interest in playing other losers.

"Sure I'm sure," he said in exasperation. It was bad enough having to play with his own sister without also having to explain every single thing to her as they went along. "Angie, we've won only one match so far, that first one we played against Andrew Munson and his mother. And that was mainly because of Andrew getting stung by a bee."

"Well, some of the others were close," Angie pointed out.

"Close is no cigar," Steve said crossly, and stomped back to the baseline. "Ready?" he called to Sally across the net.

"Ready as I'll ever be," Sally replied, tucking a long strand of butterscotch-colored hair behind one ear and dipping her knees slightly in her version of a receiver's crouch.

Steve bounced the ball twice, then tossed it high—too high, he realized; his timing was really off today—and flung all his weight at it along the axis of his outstretched arm and racket. The ball slammed into the top of the net, just missing Angie's shoulder. "Hey, watch it!" she said, turning to glare at him.

Just get the ball *in*, Steve instructed himself. He served again, more cautiously, and the ball landed safely in the middle of the service court. Sally hit a weak forehand that barely floated over the net, giving Angie plenty of time to step sideways and slap the ball back—not right at Sally, but at an angle between Sally and Dr. North, an even better shot; in fact a winner for sure.

"Yours," yelled Dr. North. To Steve's astonishment, Sally went pounding along the baseline behind her father, swung her racket wide, and whacked a backhand hard down Steve's alley. Taken by surprise, he lunged at the ball, caught it with the frame of his racket instead of the strings, and watched it carom high above the court and over the fence into Heron Lake.

"I got it!" yelled someone in a canoe, paddling into the reeds below the bank.

Angie was laughing. "That's the most running I've ever seen Sally do," she told Steve, tossing him one of the remaining balls.

"Was that in?" Sally called, shading her eyes. "Mine, I mean." She was breathless but looked pleased with herself.

"Yeah," Steve told her reluctantly. "It hit the line." To Angie he said, "That was a good shot, the one you hit. Do that again, okay?"

"But we lost the point," she objected.

4

"That was just a fluke. Still, maybe we should keep the ball away from Sally's backhand," Steve said thoughtfully. "Hit it to her forehand instead. Actually, I don't think I've ever seen Sally hit a backhand before."

Angie herself didn't like hitting backhands much, at least not up at the front of the court before the ball even had a chance to bounce. Dr. North returned Steve's serve with a drive over the center of the net, well within her reach; but at the last moment she hesitated and backed off. Steve had to scramble to get to the ball and couldn't do anything with it except hit it back to Dr. North.

"No, stay there!" he yelled to Angie as Dr. North lofted the ball high over her head. "I'll get it."

He sped back into the corner behind Angie, skidded to a stop as the ball bounced, concentrated fiercely on keeping his eye on it, and hit it crosscourt to Sally. Good, a forehand—she'd either hit the ball into the net or just poop it over, giving Angie a chance to smack it back. Except that Angie wasn't at the net anymore; she was backpedaling toward the baseline, not looking where she was going . . . about to run right into him, in fact.

Their feet tangled, they clutched at each other for balance. Sure enough, Sally hit a soft little shot that just dropped over the net and died. There was no one there to hit it back.

"If you'd stay where I tell you—" Steve said to his sister, seething.

"Well, but you said we should both always play up or

both be back," Angie protested. "That's one thing I do remember."

"But I was coming back up to the net after I hit the ball!"

"Well, how was I supposed to know that?" She tossed her feathery white-blond curls. "I'm not a mind reader, you know."

"You don't even *have* a mind," Steve told her in despair. "All right, forget it, just get me that other ball, will you? And for Pete's sake, stay up at the net this time, whatever happens."

Angie went sulkily to do his bidding, dragging her toes and muttering under her breath that it wasn't her fault they had only two balls now.

"Fifteen–forty," Steve announced from the baseline.

"Match point, I believe," Dr. North said mildly.

"Right," said Steve, and served an ace to Sally. At least it counted as an ace; Sally seemed to be giggling at something and swung at the ball only after it had gone by.

"Sorry," she said. "I was watching them get that other ball out of the water—all covered with green gunk with this long weed hanging down, like a shrunken head in a monster movie."

Steve beckoned his partner back to midcourt. "Okay, Angie, now we've got a chance," he said in an urgent undertone. "We get this next point, and then we're at deuce, and then all we have to do is win two more points and the games'll be three–five."

Angie was not impressed by this scenario. "Deuce is

so boring," she complained. "It always goes on and on."

Steve ignored this unworthy remark. "Now, look," he went on, "try to act like you really mean business at the net this time, okay? You know, lean forward and waggle your racket, stuff like that. I'm going to serve to Dr. North's backhand if I can, and if you distract him enough, maybe he'll hit it out or in the net."

"Just as long as he doesn't hit it to my backhand," Angie said darkly.

He didn't; instead, he returned the serve to her right, a looping shot down the alley. It was a stretch for Angie, but she was quick when she wanted to be, and somehow she got her racket on the ball and flicked it back over the net . . . right at Dr. North, who angled it cleanly between Steve and Angie for a winner.

"Oh, no!" Steve groaned. "Angie, that ball was going *out!*"

"Which ball?"

"The one you hit, dummy. It was out by a mile!"

"No, it wasn't, and don't call me that." Angie turned on her heel.

"Game, set, and match," announced Dr. North. There was a little spattering of applause from the sidelines as the players gathered at the net to shake hands. Angie refused to shake Steve's like you were supposed to do.

"I thought you two were beginning to get it together there," Dr. North said with a chuckle as they walked off the court. "Lucky for us you didn't, eh, Sal? Well, now, let's just see where we're at." He went over to the tree to pencil in the score and study the rest of the draw.

Steve slung his racket down on the grass and sprawled beside it. Angie went to get a Coke from the trestle table set up alongside the wide dirt driveway that led to the lodge, not offering to bring him one. "Too bad, kids," their mother said from her low chair next to Aunt Marge's. "You really played quite well."

"No, we didn't," Steve told her stonily.

He saw Aunt Marge give his mother a warning look. "Oh, well, brother and sister can be a tricky combination," she said lightly. "Even trickier than parent and child. Speaking of which, how on earth did Ed North ever persuade Sally to get out on a tennis court? I haven't seen her move around that much since she was a toddler."

Angie returned with her Coke. "He promised he'd let her pierce her ears if she'd play in the tournament. Sally's crazy about earrings. She wanted him to do it himself—yuck—but he said he was a baby doctor, not a what-do-you-call-it, a surgeon, and he wasn't going to be responsible for having his only child die of blood poisoning."

"Who's up next?" someone called, looking at the empty court.

"We are," said Mrs. Kirby, unfolding her tall, athletic frame from the chair beyond Aunt Marge's and stripping the cover from one of her three rackets. "But I don't know where our opponents are—the younger Lambert girl and her boyfriend. Anyone seen them?"

One of the off-duty waitresses said she thought they

were over at Great Harriman, sunbathing out on the raft. Dr. North, flushed with success, said, well, why didn't he and Sally take on Mrs. Kirby and her partner right now, seeing they'd be playing each other sooner or later, anyway? He wasn't all that tired, and neither was Sally. Sally looked dubious at this, but followed him out onto the court, tucking the tail of her shirt back into her white shorts. No one said you had to wear white to play in the tournament, but most people did.

Steve watched moodily as the match got under way. The Kirbys, younger and fitter than most of the other adult guests, were generally acknowledged to be the best tennis players at Potter's Lodge; but in the spirit of the tournament, they didn't play together as partners. This year Mr. Kirby was teamed with Wanda Munson. Wanda was a better player than she looked, fast on her feet and good at anticipating the flight of the ball. At least she was whenever she wasn't worrying about getting tennis elbow or about how Mr. Kirby ought to be wearing a safety guard over his glasses. Wanda had a lot of weird hang-ups, in Steve's opinion.

Mrs. Kirby, on the other hand, had elected to play with Hugh Curtis, which was a little like having a Mexican jumping bean for a partner. Hugh said he'd had two years of tennis lessons, and maybe he had. The way he flung himself around the court, Steve thought he might just as well have studied bullfighting or break dancing.

They'd been doing quite well as a team, though— mainly, Steve saw now, because Mrs. Kirby really understood tactics and made sure Hugh understood them too. Whenever it was her turn to serve, Hugh stopped bouncing around and stayed glued to the net— practically resting his chin on it, in fact—and even though he just poked at the ball excitedly when it came his way, hitting it on the throat of his racket as often as not, they won a lot of points on sheer surprise. Moreover, they were careful to keep the ball away from Dr. North, hitting it monotonously over and over again to Sally in the backcourt.

"See?" Steve said to Angie, who was sitting on the grass a few yards away. "Sally's getting all sweaty now, like she hates, and Dr. North is losing his concentration." As he spoke, Dr. North backed up to hit an overhead, smashed it into the net, and groaned loudly. The last overhead he'd tried had sailed way over the baseline and struck the fence. "And they figured out about Sally's backhand, so all she's getting to hit is forehands."

Angie shrugged. She still wasn't speaking to him. Angie rarely got really mad at him, but when she did, it was as if Steve had become invisible—as if she'd flung a magic net over him, like some character in a fairy tale.

"It's not winning I care about so much," Steve insisted to her profile. "I just think you should try to do things *right*."

His mother overheard this remark and frowned at him. When the game ended and the players were changing sides—it was already three–love for Hugh and Mrs. Kirby—she leaned forward in her chair and said,

"Steve, just relax, can't you? The tournament is supposed to be fun! Your father and I suggested you and Angie play together only because we thought you'd have a good time and maybe learn something about doubles."

"*I* learned," Steve muttered. "But she didn't. She wouldn't."

"Steve has fun only if he's in charge," Angie told her mother coldly. "He doesn't want a partner, he wants a slave."

"Oh, you two—" Mrs. Hyatt looked at her children and sighed.

"This is dumb," Steve said, pushing himself to his feet. "Who cares about the stupid tournament, anyway? It's no fun playing a sport if you have to be *nice* to everyone all the time. I've got better things to do."

Chapter 2

As usual when he was mad about something, Steve sought out his cousin Gus. Well, at home in Connecticut he couldn't seek Gus out exactly, since Gus lived sixty miles away in New York City and wasn't much for talking on the phone. But somehow just thinking about Gus always made Steve feel better. It was the calm way Gus listened—just nodding his head or shrugging once in a while; and then, after a pause to make sure you were done, changing the subject. Gus wasn't a confrontation-type person, except maybe when it came to fish. One of the best things about summer vacations in Vermont, Steve considered, was having Gus around to tell things to.

Since it was a bright, still afternoon, thus the wrong time and weather for fishing on Heron Lake, Steve decided Gus was probably over at the big lake, Great Harriman. Jogging along the broad, shady trail through the woods, he also decided maybe he wouldn't make a big deal about the tennis thing, after all. It might sound like sour grapes, even if that wasn't really the point. He'd just tell Gus that he and Angie were out of the tournament, and then they could plan something fun, like going for a hike or a bike ride or helping Pierre paint shutters over behind the staff dormitory.

The big lake glimmered wide and blue through the trees. Steve emerged into the sunlight of the grassy picnic area and stood looking around. A couple of little kids were paddling in the shallows down by the narrow beach, watched over by a baby-sitter. Fifty yards off-shore, the raft rode low in the water under the prone bodies of several teenagers, among them Kelly Lambert and her boyfriend. Steve thought of yelling to them that they were supposed to be playing tennis, but decided against it. Everyone was always telling him not to be so bossy. So okay, if they wanted to default, that was their business.

He walked out onto the broad granite ledge that overhung the water and counted the rowboats drawn up farther along by the boathouse. They were all there. Maybe Gus was casting up along the shoreline some-where. Steve was about to turn away when he spotted his cousin's neat, dark head—like an otter's, someone had once said—over on the far side of the boathouse slip. He was sitting down in a fold of the rock, intent on something in his hands.

"You don't have to be quiet," he said as Steve

approached, after picking his way over the rough ground behind the boathouse with a wary eye for nettles. "I'm just tying a fly."

Steve saw with respect that this one really did look quite a bit like an actual fly; Gus was getting better. He sat down and took off his tennis shoes and socks, then as an afterthought shucked off his shirt too—it was hot here, with the sunlight winking off the water in millions of tiny silver fish scales. Only then did he lean back on his elbows and say casually, "Well, we lost. No more boring tennis for this year."

"Who to?" Gus asked without looking up.

"Sally and her father." Gus's brown fingers paused a moment. "Dr. North is pretty good," Steve added, and hoped he hadn't sounded defensive. "But now they're getting beaten by Hugh and Mrs. Kirby. I know," he said, though Gus hadn't opened his mouth, "you wouldn't think Hugh could even swing a tennis racket without braining himself or dislocating his shoulder or something. But in a way, he sort of knows what he's doing. 'Course that's mainly because of Mrs. Kirby. I don't know, though. . . ." He frowned out at the water, then surprised himself by saying, "Maybe I'll sign up for tennis lessons when we get home, like Dad's been wanting me to do."

Gus nodded. Steve lay back and closed his eyes, listening to the gentle lisping of the water, and felt himself relax. Funny how comfortable hard old rock could be to lie on, at least for a little while. After a pause Gus said, "Mr. Kirby was down here a while ago with that dog of his, trying to teach it to swim."

"I thought dogs were born knowing how. Like an instinct or something."

"Not this one." Gus gave the grunt that, with him, passed for a laugh. "He kept trying to drink the water, like maybe if he swallowed enough of it, the lake would go away and stop bothering him. That's one dog that knows absolutely nothing."

Steve slapped at an insect buzzing around his bare shoulder, felt his palm connect, and sat up to inspect the victim. "Hey, a fly, a big one. Looks just like the fly you're trying to make." He picked up the corpse between his thumb and forefinger and studied it more closely. "It's dead, all right, but it's not even squashed. Looks good as new." An idea struck him. "Hey, where's your rod? Let's put it on the hook and see if it catches anything."

Gus looked at him blankly. "Use a real fly?"

"Why not? That's what you're pretending to do, right? I mean, you're trying to fool the fish into thinking a fake fly is real. So if you happen to have the real thing on hand . . ."

He held the dead fly out to Gus, who frowned and made no move to take it.

"I never heard of anyone casting with a real fly."

"So go ahead, try it," Steve urged. "It's pretty fat, see? You could probably stick the hook right through and not have to tie it on or anything." He looked around for Gus's rod and saw it leaning up against a birch tree near the boathouse. "What's the matter? You think the fish'll know it's dead? Don't they eat dead flies?" When Gus didn't say anything, he went on helpfully, "If you give it a little twitch when it lands, like you do with the fake ones, the fish'll never know the difference. Besides, it's been dead only about a minute."

Gus was getting his stubborn look. "I don't think it'd work," he said at last. "And also"—he hesitated—"it seems sort of like cheating."

"Oh, come on! Who's gonna care—the fish? The fly sure won't. In fact, we better hurry, it's starting to dry out." Steve examined the fly, whose iridescent gloss was already fading, set it down carefully, and scrambled up the bank for the rod. "You better put it on the hook, though, if it's gonna need a weight or any of those other doodads. I mean, you're the one that knows about fishing."

"Right," Gus said in a flat voice.

It was Steve's turn to frown at his cousin. "Hey, it's not like it's a *worm*, or a hunk of bacon or something. I mean, even I know that's not sporting, or whatever you call it. I just can't see going to all the trouble to make a fake fly when you already have a perfectly good dead one. If it's against the rules, then all I can say is the rules are pretty dumb."

He paused for breath, but Gus held up a hand. "Okay, okay," he said, and reached for his tackle box. "But I still say it won't work. Also, this is a lousy place to fish—no one ever catches anything down this way. You're lucky if you even get a nibble."

He fiddled with the fly for a minute, then stood up,

gave a hitch to his red swim trunks, and prepared to cast. "Here goes nothing," he said crossly.

Steve watched with more interest than he usually felt. Although he admired his cousin's skill and could see that fly casting took considerable muscular effort and coordination—the motion was a little like pitching a baseball—he thought privately it was a pretty dull sport, only a step or two up from watching paint dry. Now, a fishing derby would be something else again, one of those deals where you saw who could catch the biggest fish. But spending hours off by yourself just for the pleasure of persuading a fish to swallow a hook? Steve didn't get it. It wasn't as if Gus ever ate any of the fish he caught; he didn't even like tuna fish out of a can.

Gus cast once, twice. "Oh, this is a waste of time," he grumbled, reeling in and inspecting the now-sodden fly. He sent the line snaking out again. This time there was a streak of silver. Before the fly even landed, a fish leaped out of the water and snatched it.

"Wow! What'd I tell you?" Steve laughed, slapping his knee. "Fish heaven—the real thing for a change. Is he hooked? Come on, reel him in."

Scowling, Gus did so. "He's just a little one," he said. "No fight."

"So? At least it worked." Steve watched as Gus carefully removed the hook from the gills and tossed the fish back into the lake. With an agitated wriggle, it disappeared. "Give him a year or so to grow up, and then try him with another dead fly," Steve advised with a grin. "He's probably spoiled for the fake stuff now."

Gus was silent, securing his line.

"Hey, maybe you could get one of the little kids to catch flies for you," Steve suggested. "Andrew Munson, for instance. That's just the kind of dumb project he'd probably like."

Gus looked at him stonily. "You think just about everyone's dumb except you—right, Steve?"

Steve was taken aback by his tone. "Oh, come on, I was just kidding."

"No, you weren't."

He considered this, feeling uneasy under Gus's hard stare. "Hey, Andrew's a nice enough little kid, but you've got to admit he's not exactly an intellectual giant."

"That's not what I'm talking about. It's the way you're so sure you're *right* all the time."

"Well, I was right about the fly, wasn't I? I mean, you didn't even want to try it."

"And now you're the expert fisherman, I suppose." Gus shook his head and began packing up his tackle box.

"No! I don't know anything about fishing, you know that. I just thought it was logical to use a real fly, that's all. In fact, I bet that's how fly-fishing got started. Sure, it must've been. Remind me to look that up in one of those books in the lodge—you know, that shelf in the corner where they keep all the books about fish and birds and wildflowers and—"

"Right," Gus interrupted, snapping the lid shut. He picked up his rod and turned away. "I don't want to keep on hearing about it, okay?"

"Okay," Steve agreed with a baffled look at Gus's skinny brown back. "Boy, you're in a really bad mood today, you know that?"

"I was doing all right until you came along," Gus told him, and stalked away.

Steve thought of calling after him to remind him about the nettles behind the boathouse—Gus was barefoot—but decided against it. The heck with him, if he was going to be so touchy about someone else actually having an idea or two about his precious fishing. Steve stretched out on the rock again and tried to think about something pleasant, like winning the canoe race again this year, or soccer practice starting up when he got home. But sure enough, he was uncomfortable after only four or five minutes, a knob of granite grinding into his lower spine, a hollow developing in the wrong place beside his left shoulder blade. It was hot too; what little breeze there'd been seemed to have died away. Maybe he'd take a swim. Sure, a long, cold swim was probably just what he needed to wash away the sort of itchy feeling that had been growing in his mind.

He stood up and saw the swimming area was deserted now. The sitter had evidently marched her charges back through the woods, and the yelling and splashing he'd heard a few minutes before must have been the teenagers swimming in from the raft. You weren't supposed to go swimming on your own, not unless you were an adult. Still, who was going to know?

Steve looked down at his tennis shorts, thinking there might be a pair of swim trunks he could borrow in the boathouse annex. But no, that was too much trouble; he'd just go in in his shorts and take time to dry off afterward. In fact—he hesitated, looking across the quiet expanse of the lake, the trees on the far shore hazy and blue with heat against the rounded green hump of Mount Levêque beyond—he'd just dive in off the rocks here, not bother walking around to the beach. As for staying inside those dumb ropes with their bleach-bottle floats . . . well, again, who was around to see?

He hit the water in a flat racing dive, trying not to recoil at the icy slap of it against his chest and stomach, and kicked his way rapidly into deeper water, not sure what might lie underneath in the way of rocks or weeds. About twenty yards out, he let his legs down gingerly and treaded water while he picked out a mark to swim to. There was a gap in the timber on the far shore just opposite him, either a logging trail or a firebreak; he'd head for that and turn around when he was level with the tallest of the scraggly pine trees that fringed Silver Beach way off to his left, at the south end of the lake.

About three hundred yards, Steve figured. Okay, backstroke for a hundred yards, freestyle for the next hundred, and then maybe the butterfly if his breath held out. You needed to keep moving in water as cold as this.

He'd completed this program and was resting a moment, floating on his back, when he heard a creak of oarlocks and someone yelling his name. Sitting up, Steve saw one of the Potter's Lodge rowboats advancing toward him, propelled over the water in rapid, angry strokes by Ray Wallace, manager.

Oh, great. What was Ray doing over at Great Harriman at this time of day? Even from a distance, the back of Ray's neck looked red and wrathful. From feeling pleasantly tingly and limp, Steve's limbs felt suddenly heavy and numb. He forced himself to swim toward the boat, each stroke an effort, like dragging himself through wet cement.

"Get in," was all Ray said. His normally genial features were clenched into a scowl that made a heavy black bar of his eyebrows.

"I'd just as soon swim back," Steve told him, though his teeth were beginning to chatter. "I mean, I'm not tired or anything."

"Get in," Ray repeated.

It isn't all that easy to haul yourself out of deep water into a rowboat, even a flat-bottomed one, especially when no one offers you a hand. After a few heaves, Steve managed it, scraping his stomach and almost losing his tennis shorts in the process. He landed in an undignified heap on the bottom. Ray watched grimly, steadying the boat with the oars. Only when Steve was seated dripping in the stern did he speak again. "Just what did you think you were going to do?" he inquired in an ominously mild voice. "Swim across the lake?"

Steve was offended. "No way," he protested. "I know better than to try that. It must be a mile, at least. Well, I could probably swim a mile," he conceded, "but not two miles, over and back, not with the water this cold. I was just about to turn around," he assured Ray. "I had a mark all picked out so I wouldn't go too far. About three hundred yards out and three hundred back, so let's see, about a third of a mile, total. Well, not quite, I guess. Six hundred yards . . ."

But Ray wasn't interested in finer calculations. "That's about a third of a mile you're not supposed to swim at all," he said icily. "We have a few rules around here, Steve, in case you've forgotten." Steve hung his head. "How do you think I felt," Ray went on, starting to row, "showing some new people around, telling them about our nice sandy-bottomed swimming area and saying no, we didn't have a lifeguard but we did have certain safety rules everyone observed, like not swimming alone and staying inside the ropes unless there's a boat with you." He chopped savagely at the water with the oars. "And then I look out and see you splashing away, right out in the middle of the lake!"

He paused for breath. Steve looked past his shoulder at the shore, where he could now see a whole bunch of people standing out on the rocks, shading their eyes and looking in their direction.

"Wow," he said. "Who are all of them?" He always checked the blackboard in the lodge office for new arrivals, and he couldn't remember anyone scheduled to come in today, let alone a party of this size.

"People who were driving by and decided to check the place out," Ray answered testily. He turned in his seat and produced a big smile for the benefit of the watchers. "No problem!" he called. "You head on back, why don't you? I'll be along in a few minutes." To Steve he said, "I told them I'd given you special permission for a distance swim, and just thought I'd check on how you were doing."

"Driving by from where?" Steve asked. Potter's Lodge wasn't exactly on a beaten path in this remote northeastern corner of Vermont.

"I don't know, Montreal, maybe. Probably they were lost. Now, listen to me, Steve—"

"All in one car?"

"No, in two cars. Two vans, actually. A big family, name of Erskine, said they always travel together." Ray glared at him. "Stop trying to distract me."

"I'm not," Steve defended himself. "I'm just interested."

"Okay, you're interested. *I'm* interested in what your parents will have to say when I tell them about this little escapade."

"Do you have to?" Steve gave him an imploring look. "I know I broke the rules, but I'm a good swimmer, Ray, you know that, and I didn't go any farther than I knew I could, from doing laps in pools."

"Be that as it may," Ray said, a phrase Steve had often heard him fall back on when he couldn't think of an argument. Then he thought of one. "What if a speed-boat had come along and run you down?"

"There weren't any around," Steve said. "I checked."

Ray heaved a sigh that strained the buttons of his Hawaiian shirt, a flowery blue-and-yellow number he sometimes wore in hot weather. He was putting on weight around the middle, Steve observed, probably from all the good Vermont butter that Terence, the young chef, used in his cooking. "The whole point about a speedboat, Steve, is that it's *fast*. It can come at you out of nowhere."

"Well, not quite out of nowhere. And anyway, they hardly ever come down to this end of the lake, except sometimes on weekends, with water-skiers."

Ray sighed again. His grip on the oars had slackened. Steve noticed that the water he'd brought into the boat was beginning to seep into the toes of Ray's polished loafers. "Want me to row?" he offered.

"No!" Ray straightened and gave a mighty thrust of the oars that shot them almost half the remaining distance to shore.

"Well, hey, you don't have to yell at me. I was just trying to help."

"Steve the helper," Ray said between his teeth, looking over his shoulder to check his steering. "Just out of curiosity, Steve, has anyone ever succeeded in winning an argument from you?"

Steve thought about it. "My parents, I guess. And teachers sometimes."

Ray muttered something under his breath that sounded like, "God help your teachers." He didn't speak again, only grunted when Steve said he'd take care of putting the oars away so Ray could go catch up with the Erskines. Nor did he respond when Steve asked where he'd put them all if they decided to stay.

"In Pine Grosbeak and Catbird, I guess," Steve said, answering his own question aloud; he'd long ago memorized all the bird names of the cabins. "They're the only empty ones that're big enough. Too bad they're so far away from each other. Wait, though—the Hursts are leaving tomorrow, aren't they? So then some of the Erskines could go in Brown Thrasher, that's only one cabin away from Catbird. And if it's too noisy for Mr. Jeffries, being in between, maybe he could move out of Nuthatch into Merganser. Well, he's pretty deaf, so probably the Erskines wouldn't bother him, but that nurse he's got this year is really cranky. . . . Did Hal ever get around to fixing that stair railing in Merganser?"

But Ray was already stamping off toward the trail. Steve looked after him thoughtfully. He decided Ray probably wouldn't get around to saying anything to his parents, after all. Ray's wife, Nora, would have, if she'd been the one to catch him. So would Steve himself, if he'd been in charge and found a kid swimming out of bounds. In fact, given the chance, Steve was sure he could have done a pretty good job of running Potter's Lodge and Family Camp all by himself.

Chapter 3

*A*ngie still wasn't speaking to Steve at dinnertime, and Gus didn't have much to say, either—but then, he never did. When someone asked how his day's fishing had gone, he gave Steve a black look that dared him to say anything about the dead fly, then answered tersely that he hadn't caught much of anything.

Steve wasn't bothered. There was roast beef for dinner, his favorite, and also the new arrivals to study. From his seat against the inner wall, he had a good view of the two tables occupied by the Erskines across the dining room, in the right-hand corner Nora reserved for transients because it was apt to be stuffy and get the cooking smells. Steve figured out there was a middle-aged father and mother, or rather grandfather and grandmother, since the little girl in the high chair seemed to belong to one of the two pairs of grown sons and their wives. You could tell it was the sons who were

Erskines because they were large and broad shouldered and jolly looking, like their parents. Then there was a college-age son and his pretty auburn-haired girlfriend (Steve decided she was a girlfriend and not a wife from the way she kept leaning over and whispering things in his ear). The remaining member of the party was a boy about Steve's age. He didn't look much like the other Erskines, being rather pale and plump, with a round face and glasses, but Steve decided he had to be the youngest son, since he was too old to belong to either of the married couples.

"I see our ranks have swelled," Uncle Maury said in his laconic lawyer's voice, following Steve's glance. "Could be a real bonanza for Potter's. The occupancy rate hasn't been all that great this year," he added to Steve's father across the table.

"*If* they decide to stay," Steve said, and told everyone as much as he knew about the Erskines.

"Well, they seem to be having a good time," his mother said, wincing a little as the senior Mr. Erskine's laugh boomed out over the room. "Heavens, they are *big*, aren't they? But at least not all wearing matching sweatshirts and baseball caps, like that group that came off a bus last year for lunch."

"Oh, yes, the barbershop quartet people who'd been on a canoe trip," said Aunt Marge. "Remember how they serenaded us with 'I Know a Green Cathedral' before they left?"

They laughed. A fact of life to which Steve had long

since become resigned was that his mother and her sister were snobs about things like people's clothes and table manners and taste in music and way of shaking hands. Steve himself was more interested in whether a person was smart or good at sports or knew a whole lot about something—an attitude that was fortunately shared by his father and Uncle Maury.

"Well, maybe we'll be able to get the roof fixed now," Mr. Hyatt said, helping himself to horseradish sauce. "I doubt it'll make it through another winter. And do something about a new freezer too."

"The roof?" Steve said. But just then Mrs. Rowan and her granddaughter, Rita Crawford, stopped by the table on their way out of the dining room, and the conversation turned to a pileated woodpecker Mrs. Rowan thought she'd seen that afternoon, flapping through the woods beyond the stables. Had anyone else spotted it?

Mrs. Rowan was a dedicated bird-watcher; indeed, it was she who'd named the cabins, in her role as a descendant of Ephraim Potter, the lumber tycoon who'd developed the camp originally as his own private hunting and fishing preserve. In recent years, the money he'd left to keep it going hadn't been nearly enough, even combined with the fees paid by the guests, so some of the regulars, including the Hyatts and the Jacobsons, had banded together and formed a corporation they'd put some of their own money into.

Steve's father was fond of saying that Potter's was run on a shoestring—an old, frayed shoestring. Certainly no one minded the way things were sort of run-down and shabby, if only because this discouraged the kind of people who went in for glossy Technicolor vacations, as Steve's mother put it, complete with saunas and piped music and cocktail lounges. But something as basic as the lodge roof . . .

"We'll see you later at bingo, won't we?" Aunt Marge was saying as Mrs. Rowan and Rita started to move on.

"Oh, I suppose so." Mrs. Rowan made a little face. "Do you know, in all these years, I've never once held a winning card? What are the odds of that happening? I wonder. You'd think the law of averages would have worked in my favor by now."

Steve was about to explain the difference between a mean and an average when Rita said, "Oh, well, like they say, unlucky in cards, lucky in love," and then flushed an unbecoming brick red. She had the kind of telltale freckled skin that often goes with sandy hair. "I'm sorry, Gran, I didn't mean—"

"Of course you didn't, dear," Mrs. Rowan said briskly. "And even if you did, who knows, you may well be right. Well, now, we'd better run along if you're going to have time to do your archery practice before bingo."

There was a little silence at the table as Rita trailed her grandmother out through the glass doors into the high-raftered main room of the lodge. Rita's shoulders were still hunched in embarrassment on either side of the long braid that hung down her back like an exclamation point. "Love?" Angie said, and lowered her voice hastily as her mother frowned at her. "Mrs. Rowan?"

"When she was younger, I think Rita meant," Aunt Marge said, looking thoughtful. The whereabouts and even identity of Mrs. Rowan's husband was a longstanding Potter's mystery. No one knew whether she'd been widowed, divorced, or just separated from him—except possibly for Pierre, the elderly handyman and former guide. He'd known Mrs. Rowan since she was a child. Steve's mother had once tried to draw him out on the subject in her best Vassar College French, but Pierre had pretended not to understand her accent. Nor did anyone know what had caused the rift between Mrs. Rowan and her two daughters, whom some of the older guests remembered from years past. Rita was the only relation to visit Mrs. Rowan in recent memory, traveling alone from her home out in Colorado.

Right now, though, Steve was more interested in Mrs. Rowan's bingo problem. He said something about it to Gus as they went down the path to the rec house after dinner; Gus was better at math than he was. At first he thought Gus was still mad at him and wasn't going to answer, but it seemed he was just thinking. "She's got to win sooner or later," he said finally. "I mean, it's not one of those deals that can go on into infinity."

"Well, but what about now?" Steve said. "Mrs. Rowan doesn't exactly *have* until infinity."

Gus shook his head. They continued to ponder the matter while they helped Ray set up the trestle tables in the big square room lined with windows open to the soft night air. Ray greeted Steve with a rather distant nod but, as Steve had anticipated, soon relaxed into his normal affability. A natural host, Ray always liked to feel everyone was having a good time.

"I know," Gus said suddenly, pausing in the act of banging open a folding chair. "Forget the math part of it, and just say Mrs. Rowan happens to be unlucky at bingo. So okay, we get her to switch cards."

"Switch cards?"

Gus's brown eyes were alight with enthusiasm; he liked Mrs. Rowan because she knew a lot of nature stuff, not just about birds but about trees and weather and animals too, even fish. "Yeah, with someone who's naturally lucky and wins a lot, like Sally or my mother or Mr. Kirby. What I mean is, we wait until they've picked their cards out of the pile and Mrs. Rowan's picked hers, and then we have them trade."

"I don't get it," Steve said.

"Well, look, suppose there's only so much bingo luck to go around, and somehow Mrs. Rowan never gets any of it. But if she swaps cards with a *lucky* person at the last minute—" Gus broke off with a frown. "I don't know, though—if all those Erskines come tonight, that might foul things up. By spreading the luck around too much, I mean. Still, it's worth a try."

Steve said it sounded like a screwy idea to him, and Gus glared at him. "Just because it isn't *your* idea—"

"No, that's not why. I mean, even if it was, I'd think it was dumb." The expression on Gus's face reminded him of what he'd said that afternoon about Steve's thinking he always knew better than anyone else. He said hastily, "But okay. I don't think it'll work, but sure,

31

let's give it a shot and see what happens."

The room began to fill up with families drifting over from the lodge, where the adults had been drinking their after-dinner coffee on the veranda. The Erskines weren't among them. Evidently they were still getting settled in Catbird and Pine Grosbeak; or maybe they didn't approve of bingo, even at a nickel a card. Sally was agreeable to the plan, and so was Aunt Marge. Mr. Kirby, tall and athletic and efficient-looking like his wife, also never one to mince words, said the whole thing sounded completely crazy to him, but sure, Mrs. Rowan was a nice lady, he'd go along with the gag. This had the effect of rallying Steve to Gus's side. In fact, since Gus was hanging back a little, as usual, Steve found himself more or less taking charge of the proceedings.

"No, no," he said to Mrs. Rowan as she stood hesitating over the stack of cards for the first game. "Just grab one the way you usually would. And Sally, you do the same. Now—one, two, three, switch!"

"Abracadabra," said Sally, handing over her card.

"It's not that I really care about winning as such," Mrs. Rowan was explaining as they bore their cards away to one of the long tables. "It's just such a *doomed* feeling, never having my numbers turn up. Well, of course, I often get four in a row, but that fifth number simply eludes me."

Steve became so interested in seeing if Gus's experiment might possibly work that he almost forgot to keep track of his own card. When Ray called out, "I nineteen," it took him a moment to realize he'd filled in his column of I's. Ray was already rattling the drum for the next number before Steve came to his senses and exclaimed, "Oh, hey, that's me. Bingo!"

"Yay, Steve," Angie said sarcastically from the next table.

As the evening progressed, Steve found himself wondering if instead of absorbing their good luck, Mrs. Rowan could somehow be transferring her bad luck to the others. Not only did she herself not win, neither Sally, Aunt Marge, nor Mr. Kirby won a game, either. This was a spooky thought that Steve rejected almost as soon as it occurred to him—for Pete's sake, he didn't *believe* in any of this stuff.

Unusually, though, he himself won once more, and Wanda Munson too held two winning cards, which wasn't normal (if anything about Wanda could be said to be normal). Even Gus won once, after a long session in which it looked as if no one was ever going to arrive at bingo; in between numbers, it was so quiet you could hear people's breathing and the beating of moths at the screens. Gus didn't look happy about his win. By the time Ray announced the last game—the one where you had to fill in your whole card—the glow was gone from his eyes and he'd relapsed into his usual glum silence.

"Oh, well," Mrs. Rowan said lightly to Sally, whose turn it was again to exchange cards with her, "I guess it just wasn't meant to be."

Wanda spoke up unexpectedly from the other end of the table. "Maybe you should have your horoscope read," she said, and shrank back a little as everyone turned to look at her. Then she lifted her pointed chin and went on earnestly. "I've been learning about astrology because it, you know, sort of tells you what to *expect*. And it could be right there in your sign that you'd never win at bingo."

Steve groaned to himself. All Wanda needed was something more to expect, given the way she already expected the sky to fall from one moment to the next. Although maybe astrology could also tell her what *not* to expect, he thought confusedly, and thus at least narrow the scope of her worries.

Rita frowned at Wanda. "Well, hey, don't give up yet, Gran," she said bracingly. "There's still one more game to go."

Mrs. Rowan eyed her card—or rather Sally's card—and gave a rueful laugh. "All twenty-five numbers? What a hope."

"All right, people," Ray called from his post at the front of the room beside the battered old upright piano, "time for Final Bingo. Two nickels for the pot this time."

Hugh Curtis dropped one of his nickels on the floor and had to scramble under a table for it, dislodging Mr. Jeffries' cane in the process and waking the old man up, which meant his nurse had to be summoned from her knitting at the back of the room to sit beside him and repeat the numbers into his hearing aid; but finally everyone was ready. Depending on the number of players still around at the end of the evening, thus the number of cards being used, Final Bingo could take a long time. Steve sighed and planted his elbows on either side of his card. If there was anything in this distribution-of-luck business, he figured he'd already used his up. In fact, by rights the winner ought to be someone at the far table, the one over by the door to the screened porch, because no one there had won all evening.

But Ray had only half emptied the drum when there was a gasp from Mrs. Rowan. "I don't believe it," she breathed, sitting back with a thump and staring down at her card. "Bingo!"

There were cheers and applause from the other players, most of whom were aware by now of the luck-transference project. Gus came to life. "Wow," he said, "you won the whole big pot!"

"I know," Mrs. Rowan said dazedly. "Or rather Sally and I did, I guess. Here, Sally, you really ought to take half of it." Mr. Kirby, shaking his head in disbelief, was already sweeping coins along the table toward her with his long arms.

"Hold it," Ray called. "We have to check the numbers first, remember? Hold on to your cards, everyone."

Gus took Mrs. Rowan's card up to the front of the room, and he and Ray began going through the numbers. People were scraping back their chairs, chatting, gathering up belongings. Steve wandered over to the piano, where Ray and Gus had reached the G numbers. "G fifty-nine," he heard Gus say, and then, after a slight pause, "G fifty-one."

Steve looked over his shoulder. "Hey, that's not a one,

it's a seven. See, the card's sort of worn away there, but that's definitely a seven."

Frowning, Gus ran his thumb over the spot on the pasteboard where the thin top layer of paper had been scuffed away. "G fifty-seven, then," he told Ray.

"Not called," Steve said positively. "I know, because that was one of the numbers I was trying to get. Mrs. Rowan must've made a mistake." As Gus glowered at him and Ray searched in vain for G 57 among the used numbers, he added, "It's easy enough to do unless you look at it really close. I mean, I know she didn't do it on purpose."

Gus said in a furious undertone, "So just shut up about it, can't you?"

"Well, no," Steve said, surprised. "That wouldn't be fair."

Ray looked at him helplessly for a moment, then turned and held up a hand for silence. "Seems we don't have a winner, after all," he announced to the room at large, and explained what had happened.

"Oh, dear, how embarrassing," Mrs. Rowan said after the little stir had died down, examining the card. "Of course, I see now that's a seven, not a one. I ought to have been wearing my glasses—pure vanity not to. I'm so sorry, everyone!" As people hitched their chairs back into place and bent over their cards again, she added cheerfully, "Well, at least all I'm missing is one number. I may win yet."

But of the next nine numbers called, none was G 57, and on the tenth, it was the older Lambert girl who called out "Bingo!" from her seat—sure enough—at the far table.

"What a good thing you spotted that, Steve," Mrs. Rowan said pleasantly on her way to the door with Aunt Marge. "I'm disappointed, of course, but I certainly wouldn't want to win on an *error*. Maybe Wanda's right, and bingo's just not in my stars. On the whole, though," she added with a laugh and a twinkle of her blue eyes, "I think I'd just as soon not have my horoscope read. Half the fun in life is hoping, don't you think?"

Steve was looking after her and thinking what a classy lady she was when he became aware of several pairs of hostile eyes fixed on him. "Can't you ever keep your big mouth shut?" Angie demanded. Sally said, "Yes, that was really mean of you, Steve."

"Mean?" Steve was outraged. "Come on, was it my fault Mrs. Rowan read the number wrong? I wanted her to win just as much as you did, in fact I thought maybe all the luck we'd been trying to give her was finally coming together in one big lump."

"No, you didn't," Gus said bitterly. "You thought it was a dumb idea, remember? So when you saw a chance to ruin it, you grabbed it."

Steve stared at him. "You mean you wouldn't have told Ray that wasn't G fifty-one? You knew it was a seven, I saw you looking at it."

Gus hesitated a moment, then said firmly, "No, I wouldn't have."

"Well, I just don't understand you, then." Steve shook his head and turned away.

"Too bad," Gus said. "Because I guess we understand you okay. Good old Steve, always has to be *right*."

"Yes, it must get to be sort of boring after a while," Sally remarked sweetly. "So predictable."

"It's boring to live with, that's for sure," Angie told her.

Steve smashed a couple of folding chairs together and carried them over to a corner. By the time he'd stacked them and returned for more, the others had left. Only Ray remained, bundling up the bingo cards and returning the plastic counters to their box. Once again, he wasn't quite meeting Steve's eye.

Chapter 4

Steve spent a restless night in the back bedroom of Cedar Waxwing, which was about the size of his clothes closet at home. Ordinarily he didn't mind these cramped quarters; in fact it was sort of fun being able to reach out and touch the bare plank walls on either side as he lay in bed, and even hang his legs out the window if he felt like it.

Tonight, though, the little room felt close and airless, and the clean wood smell he usually inhaled with pleasure made him think instead of a coffin. Every time he closed his eyes, he seemed to see a circle of reproachful faces looking down at him—Gus and Ray, Angie and Sally, his parents, even Wanda for some reason. Also there was a cricket in the room, either that or just outside it. Steve tried to track it down with his flashlight, but every time he switched on the beam, the cricket froze into silence. Toward dawn, a little breeze

39

sprang up that he couldn't exactly feel but could hear whispering through the hemlocks behind the cabin. He sighed, turned over, and fell into a dreamless sleep from which he awoke refreshed three hours later, the faces forgotten. Steve never needed much sleep, possibly because he considered it a waste of valuable time.

The first thing to do, he decided, pulling on shorts and a T-shirt and running a brush over his short blond hair, was make his peace with Gus, who with any luck would be in a better mood today. But when he got to the dining room, he found that Gus had eaten early and gone off with his father and Dr. North on an all-day fishing trip to one of the Canadian lakes. This was the kind of excursion that had to be arranged in advance, and Steve felt hurt that Gus hadn't even mentioned it to him.

Luckily, hurt feelings never interfered with Steve's appetite. He put away a bowl of cereal with fresh blueberries, four slices of bacon, and three servings of waffles drenched in the local maple syrup, which always tasted even better here than at home, though it was exactly the same syrup they took back with them to Connecticut in shiny silver tins. Then he went out onto the veranda to plan his day.

Heron Lake gleamed blue and inviting in the morning sunshine, a light mist still wreathing the opposite shoreline. Maybe he'd take a canoe and go check out the beaver dam at the north end, something he hadn't done yet this year. But as he looked down at the little dock, Steve saw Hugh Curtis clambering into one of the rowboats. Typically, Hugh had neglected to put the oars in first and now had to reach back to the dock for them, a maneuver that widened the gap between the dock and boat and almost spilled him into the water. Steve sighed. Hugh would be sure to follow him, asking a lot of dumb questions and making a general pest of himself. Besides, the best canoe, the red one, was already out.

Well, maybe he'd see if Angie wanted to go on a bike ride before it got too hot. They could take the back road to Gilead, so-called, a dirt road that petered out in second-growth forest long before it got to Gilead or anywhere else. Then he remembered that Angie was due to go horseback riding this morning, also that her mood was still unfriendly—she'd arrived at the breakfast table just as he was leaving it and had barely nodded at him as she slid into her chair.

Steve turned to look at the outdoor blackboard on which the day's planned activities were scrawled in Ray's big, looping hand. Today there was a picnic hike up Harriman Mountain, something he'd done a million times before, and tonight a slide show in the rec house—pictures of a recent trip to Russia taken by the Curtises, Hugh's uncle and aunt. Actually, Steve might have been interested if the trip had been taken by anyone else; he'd already decided to learn Russian when he got to college, since he was sure that was where the action was going to be, businesswise, by the time he grew up. (Steve planned to make a million dollars before he was twenty-five, after which he'd turn his attention to something more interesting.) Knowing the Curtises, though, he figured the pictures would just be of boring scenery taken through a blurry tour-bus window.

Screek, groan, thump. Down on the tennis court, the heavy, rust-frilled iron roller was being manhandled over the clay by Hal, the part-time handyman who helped Pierre with the heavy work. Steve thought of the way his serve had let him down yesterday, and his backhand, too. Maybe one of his parents would hit with him for a while, before people started showing up to continue the mixed-doubles tournament—if anyone did.

He was halfway along the gravel path leading back to the cabin before he remembered his father was mad at him for leaving his racket on the grass, and his mother equally cross at the condition of his good tennis shorts.

As his steps lagged, he spotted Rita Crawford striding along the dirt road below in her cowboy boots. She had a large bow slung over her shoulder and was carrying a fistful of arrows. Steve dodged down through the trees to intercept her.

"Hey, Rita, want to have a contest?" he hailed her. "You must be getting pretty good," he added craftily, "the way you're always practicing." Steve himself had a mirrorful of blue ribbons at home from previous Potter's archery tournaments, but Rita didn't have to know that.

Rita frowned, narrowing her pale-lashed hazel eyes. Steve wondered belatedly if Rita too was down on him because of last night—Mrs. Rowan was her grandmother, after all. But it wasn't that. "I'm not into competition, remember?"

"Oh, right. Well, we wouldn't have to keep score or

anything," Steve told her (though of course *he* would, in his head). "But having someone to shoot against can give you that little extra edge, you know?"

Rita thought about this, then shook her head with a twitch of her long braid. "I don't think so. See, what I'm practicing for is rattlesnakes. I pretend the bull's-eye is a rattler on a ledge, just lying in wait for me and my horse as we come around a bend in the trail. It rears up, ready to strike, and then—pow! I put an arrow through its neck."

"Do snakes have necks?" Steve asked.

"Whatever." Rita shrugged. "Anyway, having some-one else around would probably just wreck my concentration. I'll be done in about an hour," she added politely, "if you want to take a turn then."

Steve grinned to himself as she marched on past a tall stand of fireweed and turned in at the gate of the long-grassed enclosure that served as an archery range. Wait'll he told Gus about Rita planning to make like an Indian on horseback with her bow and arrow. Actually he was pretty sure the Indians didn't bother with arrows when it came to picking off rattlesnakes; surely they just leaned down and clubbed them to death—something Rita would certainly never do, given the way she was always rescuing spiders and daddy longlegs from peo-ple's bathrooms, and wouldn't even let Steve toss a pebble at a chipmunk that was trying to raid his bag of potato chips one day over at Great Harriman.

Also, Steve had found out that Rita didn't live out in the wilds of Colorado somewhere, like you'd think from the way she acted, but just in an ordinary house in a Denver suburb—something else to tell Gus when they were back to being friends again.

For a moment he was tempted to go spy on Rita taking aim at an imaginary rattlesnake, but he dismissed the idea as being possibly dangerous—who knew if she could even control that heavyweight bow she'd picked out? Instead, with a vague idea of seeing if Sally was around and had gotten over being so sarcastic and might want to play backgammon or something, Steve angled back up the slope to the cabin path, a maneuver that sent the Kirbys' dog into one of its violent barking fits.

"Hey, pooch, it's just me," Steve said, holding out a hand. The dog was chained to the stair railing and had managed to wrap the chain around itself so many times it couldn't move more than a foot in any direction. Steve couldn't remember its name, nor did he know what combination of breeds had gone into its composition. Probably no one did, since the Kirbys had gotten it from a pound. All their friends were into fancy breeds like German pointers and Lhasa apsos, they explained scornfully; they themselves believed mutts had more personality, and besides, it was such a good feeling to know you'd saved an innocent creature from almost certain execution. For a pair of fast-track tax lawyers, as Uncle Maury described them, the Kirbys were remarkably high-minded. Of course, they came from Boston.

The dog continued to bark. "Calm down, fella," Steve urged as Mr. Jeffries' nurse appeared on the porch of Nuthatch several cabins away and shook her fist at both of them. He began trying to unwind the chain. The dog didn't seem to understand, but finally Steve got it turning around in the right direction, and at least it had stopped barking.

"Okay, now," he said. "Sit." The dog waved its sparsely plumed tail uncertainly. Steve pushed at its hindquarters. "Sit," he repeated. The dog sat, looking at him with mild brown eyes. It had a setterlike head that sort of went with the tail, though the ears were more like a terrier's.

"Oh, good, you got him quieted down." Mrs. Kirby appeared on the porch above, clutching a sheaf of papers.

"I'm afraid it was me that started him barking," Steve said apologetically, stroking the multicolored ruff of fur around the dog's neck (maybe he had some husky blood, too?)—assorted shades of brown mixed with black.

"Not necessarily. I mean, anything can. Even a beetle, if he happens to notice it suddenly. And hummingbirds drive him absolutely bananas. I think it's because he can't figure out if they're birds or insects."

Mrs. Kirby looked over at Nuthatch, where the nurse had stomped back inside, banging the screen door pointedly behind her. "That woman keeps telling me what a quiet, well-behaved dog Fritz is," she said with a frown. Fritz was Mr. Jeffries' old schnauzer. "Well, of course he is, he's on his last legs, poor thing. Not like Motley here, who's just full of life. Aren't you, boy?"

She spoke fondly, leaning over the railing, but Motley didn't turn his head. He continued to gaze at Steve in a way Steve found a bit unnerving. He wondered if

Motley could be slightly deaf. With all the racket he was always making, maybe he'd damaged his own ears, like humans could do by wearing their Walkmans turned up too loud.

Mrs. Kirby straightened, pushing up the sleeves of her pink warm-up suit. "Well, I've simply got to finish this batch of papers before Ray takes the mail over to West Eliot. Lie down, Motley—see, there's a nice patch of shade right there—and then later we'll go for a good romp."

"I could take him for a walk right now, if you want," Steve volunteered under the spell of the dog's gaze.

"Oh, would you, Steve? That would be marvelous— then I could really concentrate. Except I should warn you, Motley's more likely to take *you* for a walk than vice versa." Laughing merrily, Mrs. Kirby was in and out of the cabin in a flash with Motley's leash.

Steve took it from her, wondering what on earth had possessed him. They'd all seen what Motley could do with a leash. He'd be lucky to get a hundred yards without breaking a leg. On the other hand, he thought, maybe that wasn't really Motley's fault. The Kirbys never seemed to make any serious effort to control him, let alone discipline him.

"Just give him a good, sharp yank," Mrs. Kirby advised after Steve had detached the chain and clipped on the leash and was trying to get Motley to stand up. "He needs to know you really mean it."

For the first few yards, Steve had to drag Motley along the gravel behind him. Then Motley got the idea, and their respective positions were instantly reversed. Clearly Motley had no use for paths; he hurtled diagonally down the slope toward the road, choosing his own way around the various trees they encountered (mostly he zigged when Steve would have zagged). At the bottom, he paused for a moment to lift his leg against the Hursts' station wagon, newly washed for their departure, then shot across the road, almost yanking Steve's arm from its socket, and plunged into the fireweed—heading, it seemed, directly for the lake.

"Remember, Motley, you can't swim," Steve said breathlessly, crashing through dense pink-flowered stalks as high as his head. He couldn't even see Motley at the other end of the leash, but he could feel the ground getting spongy and damp under his feet. He hauled on the leash and dug in his heels. "Motley, stop!"

Motley did, so abruptly that Steve sat down hard in a clump of skunk cabbage. He crawled forward and found the dog with its forepaws planted on the very edge of the muddy bank, prevented from sliding into the water only by a tangle of exposed tree roots. He was also growling at something.

"Those are just water lilies," Steve told him. "Come on, Motley, this is not a good place for a walk." But Motley had spotted something else—his own master, fishing from a rowboat about twenty yards away. Steve was impressed: maybe Motley had had a destination in mind all along. But then why was he still growling?

"Oh, Motley, go away," Mr. Kirby said, and took off the slouch-brimmed fisherman's hat he was wearing.

"See, it's just me." Motley's growls erupted into barks. "He always does this to me when I'm fishing," Mr. Kirby yelled to Steve over the din. "He thinks it's me, but then when he gets close, he's not sure."

This made no sense to Steve, but he took a firm grip on Motley's collar and yelled back, "Maybe you should try taking him with you."

"Motley in a boat?" Mr. Kirby laughed heartily. "That'll be the day. Just get him away from here, will you, Steve? I'm never going to catch anything at this rate."

At the sound of Mr. Kirby's laughter, Motley had stopped barking and pricked up his ears—at least the one ear that would prick. Steve took advantage of the lull to say loudly and cheerily, "Come on, boy, let's go on with our walk." He shortened up on the leash, prepared to drag Motley away from the bank by main force if necessary; but maybe the word "walk" had finally registered. Motley offered no protest but followed Steve meekly back along the path they'd trampled through the fireweed.

"That's right," Steve said as they regained the road. "Heel, Motley." The dog gave him an inquiring look and waved his tail. "Hey, I think maybe someone must've tried to teach you that once. Heel," Steve said again experimentally. He found he was almost holding his breath as Motley continued to trot docilely beside him, all the way past the little kids' playground area to the badminton lawn, a rectangle of grass separated from the tennis court by a bed of tall yellow zinnias. Here

Steve paused and looked down thoughtfully.

"Okay, Motley," he said, and led him onto the grass. "Let's try you on some basic commands. *Sit.*" But if Motley had some dim memory of "heel," "sit" was not in his current vocabulary. Nor were "lie down" or "stay." Still, as long as he seemed to be in a tractable mood . . .

Steve tied Motley's leash to the trunk of a tree, told him he'd be right back, and dashed up to the lodge. From a side table just inside the dining room, he grabbed a handful of crackers in cellophane packets—oyster crackers, he saw they were, those little hexagonal saltines people sometimes ate with their soup (Potter's cuisine didn't run to oysters as such)—and stuffed them into his pockets. Probably the Kirbys had a box of dog biscuits in their cabin, but he didn't want to leave Motley alone long enough to go get it. One thing Steve was sure of, you couldn't train a dog without some kind of reward system.

Even though he hadn't been gone more than a minute, Motley had already wrapped his leash three times around the tree. Steve unwound him and told him to sit, giving his rump a good shove as he said the word. Motley sank down onto the grass, flopped over on his back, and waved his muddy paws playfully in the air. Steve wasn't sure he'd learned anything from this exercise, but he pulled the dog back onto his feet and gave him an oyster cracker anyway. Motley swallowed it and looked surprised. Well, it was pretty small and light, Steve thought, and gave him another. "Sit," he said again. Motley waved his tail. Steve pushed; again Motley collapsed bonelessly onto the grass. They repeated this sequence several times.

"No, Motley, that's 'lie down,'" Steve said finally, hauling Motley back onto his feet for the fourth or fifth time. He decided to change his tune. "But okay, let's say it's 'lie down' we're working on. Lie down, Motley." He gave Motley's rump a push; Motley obligingly collapsed. "*Good* dog!" Steve said in a loud, enthusiastic voice that sounded fatuous even to himself. "Now again: lie down."

This time he'd see if Motley would do it without being pushed. But Motley was distracted first by a passing butterfly, then by the crackle of cellophane as Steve tore open a fresh packet of oyster crackers. He lunged at the packet, almost nipping Steve's fingers. "No, Motley, you just had one," Steve told him sternly. "First you have to lie down." Motley was trying to nose at his pockets; it was as if he'd only just figured out where the crackers were coming from. "Lie down, Motley," Steve repeated.

Motley sank onto his haunches, his eyes fixed on Steve's pockets. "No, all the way down," Steve told him. "Lie down!" Motley continued to sit. The more Steve told him to lie down, the more stubbornly he sat and the more wooden his expression became. Steve sighed. "That's not 'lie down,' Motley, that's 'sit.' But okay, let's go back to that. We'll pretend I said 'sit.' So *sit*, Motley, that's a good dog."

Motley lay down. Steve glared at him. Motley's tail

thumped the grass; he rolled an eye at Steve, looking pleased with himself. "You are a complete bonehead, you know that?" Steve said in disgust. Then he relented, gave Motley an oyster cracker, and told him he was a good dog. Of the two of them, Steve thought resignedly, he himself was probably the more confused. "Okay, I guess you've concentrated long enough," he said, and looked around for a stick to throw. He figured it would be safe to let Motley off his leash as long as he had the crackers in his pocket.

But it appeared Motley didn't understand "fetch," either. When Steve threw the stick for him, he charged off after it and came back with a large pinecone. Well, maybe he preferred chasing pinecones. Steve pried it from his jaws with some difficulty and tossed it up in the air. Motley ignored it, wandered away across the grass, and started digging in the zinnia bed.

"Motley, no! Come here!" Motley turned his head and stared at Steve as if he'd never seen him before. "You are an *idiot*!" Steve yelled, losing patience. "Crackers, remember? Come on, Motley, you dumb dog, don't you want a cracker?" Motley went back to his digging.

"Crackers?" said a voice behind him—Mrs. Kirby, with a large manila envelope under her arm and a frown creasing the tanned skin of her forehead. "Why is Motley off his leash? What have you been doing to him?" She broke off to say, "Stop that, Motley, we don't want to ruin the pretty flowers, do we?" Motley paid no more attention to her than he had to Steve. Mrs. Kirby snatched up the leash, strode over to Motley, and snapped it to his collar. Pulling Motley over the grass behind her, she returned to Steve. "Well?"

"I was just trying to train him a little," Steve explained. "With these," he added, showing her the oyster crackers.

"Oh, for heaven's sake, all that *salt*! Poor thing, he'll be dying of thirst before long." Indeed, Motley's tongue was now hanging out, large and pink and dirt-streaked. "Really, Steve, don't you know anything about dogs?"

Steve opened his mouth to say they had two dogs at home, or rather in the boarding kennel at the moment, an Old English sheepdog and a long-haired dachshund, but thought better of it. They were probably just the kinds of dogs the Kirbys disapproved of; probably they disapproved of boarding kennels too.

"In the first place," Mrs. Kirby said more calmly, "we never feed Motley between meals, and certainly not crackers. Next thing you know, he'll be begging—such an unattractive habit in a dog." She spoke as if Motley's habits were otherwise irreproachable. "And in the second place, what do you mean, training? I thought you were taking Motley for a walk."

"I was," Steve said. "I did. But he really needs it—training, I mean. Motley doesn't know *anything*, do you realize?" Before Mrs. Kirby could speak, he hurried on. "Have you ever thought of taking him to obedience school?"

"A neighbor of ours has suggested it," Mrs. Kirby said coldly—Steve felt an immediate bond of sympathy with the neighbor—"but I'm afraid it's not our sort of thing.

I mean, what does obedience training amount to, really, but breaking a dog's spirit? And we simply couldn't bear to see that happen to Motley." She patted Motley on the top of his meek-looking head. "After all, who knows what kind of life he had before we got him, poor baby."

Steve gave it one last try, as much for Motley's sake as for his own. "Motley, lie down," he commanded. Motley waved his tail agreeably, then sat down off-balance on one haunch and began to scratch vigorously at a flea.

Chapter 5

$\mathcal{S}$teve heard a giggle behind him and spun around to find they'd collected a small audience—Kelly Lambert and her boyfriend, dressed for tennis, Ray with the mailbag slung over his shoulder, one of the Erskine wives pushing the little kid in a stroller, Sally North, and Hugh Curtis, back from his boating adventure. All were grinning broadly except for Hugh, whose mouth, as usual, hung slightly open.

Steve's ears felt hot, meaning the tips had probably turned red. With a last glare at Motley, he strode back to the lodge and stomped up the steps, ignoring the amused glances of several other watchers on the veranda. Doris, the elderly headwaitress, was just closing the glass doors to the dining room as Steve leaned in to toss the remaining packets of oyster crackers back into their wicker basket.

"What are you doing with those crackers?" she demanded.

"Putting them back," Steve said crossly. "What does it look like I'm doing?"

"Well, I don't want them—look, they're all smashed."

"No, they're not." Steve inspected the packet in his hand. "A couple of broken corners, maybe, but so what?"

"I serve fresh food in my dining room, thank you very much." Doris drew herself up, almost crackling in her crisp yellow uniform. "And who told you you could help yourself in the first place, may I ask?"

"Oh, for Pete's sake, Doris, a bunch of dumb little crackers! They're here for the guests to eat, right? And I'm a guest, in case you didn't notice." Doris regarded him grimly with her small, watery eyes. "I can help myself to the whole basketful if I want to," Steve said recklessly. "Or maybe you think I should pay extra for them? Fine, I'll ask my parents, I'm sure they'll be glad to finance my sudden cracker habit."

"I don't like your tone, young man."

"And I don't like yours," Steve told her rudely. "Besides, what do you mean, 'my dining room'? You just work here, you know."

"Right, I'll be sure to remember that in the future," Doris snapped, and closed the doors so smartly she almost caught Steve's wrist between them.

"Steve, may I have a word with you, please?"

Nora Wallace was standing in the archway that

separated the lounge from the office area, her hands on her narrow, denim-clad hips and her eyes shooting cobalt blue sparks at him. With a jerk of her chin, she motioned Steve to join her in the office. Belatedly he saw there were several older guests scattered about the big room, snoozing in armchairs or reading newspapers or working the jumbo-size jigsaw puzzle in the corner.

"I can't afford to lose Doris," Nora informed him without preamble. "I know she can be difficult, especially when her arthritis is acting up, but she's a valued member of my staff. Terence is hopeless when it comes to things like keeping track of basic supplies—he'd run out of salt and pepper if Doris didn't keep an eye on the pantry shelves. She's also a native of West Eliot, and that's an important local tie for us." Nora and Ray came from Massachusetts, Steve knew, and thus were still outlanders after fifteen summers at Potter's Lodge. "I might add that Doris is presently caring for three grandchildren whose mother has gone off to seek her fortune as a rock singer. She doesn't need any more backtalk than she probably already gets at home."

Steve felt sorry for the grandchildren, but thought better of saying so. In fact, for once in his life he couldn't think of much of anything to say. Instead, he stared glumly down at the display of Vermont crafts in the glass case below the counter—little birch-bark canoes, dishes painted with wildflowers, a folded patchwork quilt that had been there as long as Steve could remember, still pristine in its plastic bag. All the ladies admired it while also deploring its price.

"Rough morning, I gather," Nora said dryly, but her tone sounded a little friendlier. "What *was* all that about the Kirbys' dog, anyway?"

"I was just taking it for a walk," Steve muttered.

"More fool you." She went around behind the counter and began leafing through a stack of papers. "We're considering building a special cabin for Motley—his very own doghouse, on the other side of Heron Lake. Even then, it should probably be soundproofed." She paused, then said lightly, "I know Gus is off fishing, but where's Angie this morning? I thought I'd be seeing the two of you out on the tennis court."

"We're too far behind. She's going riding."

Nora gave him a thoughtful glance before she returned her attention to the papers, checking them against a list of names. After a moment, she said casually, "Actually, Steve, if you have a few minutes to spare, there's something you could do for me."

"Sure," he said with alacrity, welcoming the prospect of getting back into at least one person's good graces. "What is it?"

"These picnic lunch orders—or rather the missing picnic lunch orders. People have been lax recently about turning them in on time," Nora explained, "and if we don't get the orders by midmorning, it creates problems in the kitchen. Also I think I forgot to tell the Erskines they'd find the forms in their desk drawers. Of course, Catbird's a housekeeping cabin, so maybe they'll want to fix their own lunches." She frowned, and Steve wondered if she was thinking of the loss of revenue that would mean. "Anyway, here're some extra forms to take along in case someone needs them. Just make the rounds, would you, and collect any orders that are still out? I'd really appreciate it."

"Glad to," Steve said, and banged out the side door, reading the top form as he went. He'd never really looked at one before, since his mother always filled out his order, and anyway he usually had the same lunch— egg salad on rye, two dill pickles, a bag of potato chips, a peach and a plum, a cupcake, some peanut-butter cookies, and a thermos of milk.

There were an amazing number of blanks to check, he saw. Just for bread alone, you could choose white, whole wheat, rye, pumpernickel, or a bun, plain or sesameseed. On the bread you could have butter, margarine, mayonnaise, Miracle Whip, mustard, horseradish, or ketchup—or for that matter all of them at once, Steve thought with a grin, deciding that would be a good trick to play on Angie sometime, if he could get hold of her lunch order before their mother turned it in.

And then there were all the sandwich fillings themselves: tuna and chicken and ham and two kinds of salami, also bologna, peanut butter, jelly, peanut butter and jelly, jelly and cream cheese, olives and cream cheese—yuck—plain cream cheese on banana bread (another kind of bread!), to say nothing of a whole bunch of other cheeses: American, Swiss, cheddar, jack, and provolone, whatever that was.

By the time Steve had been in and out of Tree Swallow, Wood Thrush, and Ruffed Grouse, he'd decided there were entirely too many choices, also that Nora could probably use a computer just to deal with the picnic-lunch orders. The mother in Tree Swallow couldn't decide whether she wanted mayonnaise or Miracle Whip with her chicken sandwich, or whether to have iced tea or iced coffee. If she did have iced coffee, should she have regular or decaffeinated? She hadn't slept very well last night (Tree Swallow had a small, hot upstairs, which she was sharing with three little kids), so by lunchtime could probably use something to pick her up; on the other hand, caffeine wasn't really very good for you. . . .

The Lamberts, in Wood Thrush, had already turned in their orders, but were now considering going over to New Hampshire for lunch instead, at a new Mexican restaurant; it all depended on how Kelly and her boyfriend did in the tennis tournament. Steve said he had to know now. "Well, go find out the score, then," said Kelly's older sister, Kim, not bothering to look up from the absorbing task of painting her toenails a particularly nasty shade of orange. Steve told her if they didn't cancel their orders within the next five minutes, they'd be charged for their picnic lunches whether they ate them or not, then stamped off down the porch steps.

In Ruffed Grouse, he found Andrew Munson lying on his stomach on the braided rug in the living room, pushing some plastic monsters around. "Oh, yeah, I was supposed to bring these up to the lodge," he said, scrambling to his feet and handing Steve three neatly filled-out forms.

Steve frowned. "Where's yours? Aren't you having lunch?"

"Naw. Mom said I could do my own, now that I can read and everything, but I'm not hungry."

"Andrew, it's only nine-thirty," Steve said in exasperation. "Sure, you're not hungry now, but you will be by lunchtime."

Andrew thought about this. "Well, maybe when I get on top of Harriman Mountain I might be. I'm going on the hike," he said importantly. "Ray said I was big enough now, long as I made double knots in my shoelaces."

"Right. So you better order your picnic, or everyone else will have something to eat and you won't. What kind of sandwich do you want?" Steve asked, looking around for a pencil.

But Andrew didn't know. Nothing on the whole long list sounded good to him. Finally Steve put him down for a peanut-butter-and-jelly sandwich on white bread, an apple, and chocolate milk. Just then Wanda returned from collecting berries for her terrarium and said Andrew wasn't allowed to have chocolate milk, it gave him hives. "*Once* it gave me hives," Andrew protested. "And that might just have been my chicken pox starting." Steve erased the check mark next to chocolate milk, put one beside plain milk, and left them arguing, determined to make his escape before Wanda could tell him Andrew should have whole wheat instead of white, or a plum instead of an apple.

His last stop was Catbird. There'd been no one in

Pine Grosbeak, and now Steve saw why—all the Erskines seemed to be assembled on Catbird's wide front porch. Or rather, some of them were on the porch; others were unloading bags of groceries from one of the vans and carrying them into the cabin. Steve figured that pretty much answered the question of whether the Erskines wanted lunches fixed for them. He was turning away when he was hailed by the boy with the glasses—his name was Fred, Steve had found out.

"Oh, hey," he said, pushing himself up from the bottom step where he'd been directing traffic (and managing not to do any of the carrying, Steve noticed), "you're the kid that almost drowned over at the other lake yesterday, right?"

Before Steve could open his mouth to deny this preposterous statement, he went on earnestly. "You know, a good idea when you're swimming out a long way is to take an inner tube along—like tie a rope around it and fasten it to your ankle, see? Or even simpler, I guess, you could just tie a rope to the dock so you could haul yourself back in if you needed to. 'Course it would have to be a pretty long rope."

Steve stared at him, speechless. The boy's face beamed friendliness and concern, his round gray eyes gleaming benevolently behind the larger circles of his rather dirty glasses. Finally Steve pulled himself together. "In the first place," he said, "I wasn't drowning, just resting. In the second place, there isn't any dock over at Great Harriman. In the third place, that's just about the dumbest idea I ever heard." He turned on his heel.

"Well, you could tie the rope around a rock, then," the boy suggested to his back. "Or hey, maybe you guys should *build* a dock over at Great What's-its-name. It would be good for waterskiing. I don't water-ski myself, I'm not athletic, but my brothers are crazy about it. Except I guess there isn't any powerboat, is there, except for that old broken-down launch . . ."

Fuming, Steve marched back to the lodge. A file of horseback riders clopped by on the road below, raising soft puffs of dust. Angie was in the lead; out of the corner of his eye, Steve saw her wave to him, signaling she'd gotten over being mad, but he ignored her. As he passed Tree Swallow, the distraught mother ran out to intercept him, saying she thought she'd have regular iced coffee after all, not decaffeinated.

Steve stalked into the office, slapped the lunch forms down on the counter, and said explosively, "This place is full of idiots!" Nora turned a startled face to him from the little room beyond the counter where she was typing something. "No one around here knows their own mind," Steve informed her bitterly. "Or if they do, they change it two seconds later. Also, this menu, or whatever you call it, is completely ridiculous. That's how they drive lab rats crazy, you know—putting them in a maze with so many choices they can't decide which way to turn."

"Steve, calm down, will you?" Nora rose from the typewriter. "The only person I see going crazy around here is you! People *like* variety—it's one of the things that keeps them coming back year after year. Of course, if you stand over them and demand they make an instant decision . . ." She gave him a sharp look. "I hope you weren't rude to anyone."

"Just about all of 'em," Steve said shortly. He brushed past the end of the counter, heading for the door onto the back porch, but Nora—who could move as swiftly as a girl when she wanted to—blocked his way.

"Now, listen to me, Steve Hyatt." She was really angry now, Steve saw, her square Yankee jaw set in a flat line, her eyes as hard as blue enamel. "You're a bright, attractive boy, with lots of talent and ability going for you. But you're also going to wind up leading a very lonely life if you persist in shortchanging the rest of the human race. Other people may not be as sure of themselves as you are, but that doesn't mean they don't have their own special abilities and talents too. Why don't you devote some of your brains and energy to finding out what they are?"

She shook her head and turned away. "There's a word for the way you've been acting lately, Steve, and that's 'arrogant.' Go look it up if you don't know what it means. And now, if you'll excuse me, I'd better go deliver these picnic orders to the kitchen. I'd ask you to do it, but I'd be afraid I might not have any staff left by lunchtime."

Steve didn't have to look up the word "arrogant"; he knew what it meant. Slowly he pushed open the screen door and crossed the kitchen yard. Hal was chopping wood in the clearing behind the car shed, splitting cedar logs into smaller chunks that would fit into the cabin stoves. Steve stood watching the rhythmic rise and fall of the ax for a while, and then—more out of reflex than because he really felt much like exerting himself—offered to help.

"I could take some whacks while you rest," he said, looking at the sweat gleaming on Hal's powerful bare chest and shoulders.

"No, thanks, sonny. There's a trick to this, you know—wouldn't want you to hurt yourself."

"But I know how," Steve said, stung. "I help my dad chop wood all the time at home in Connecticut."

"Connecticut, huh." Hal puffed out his lower lip to blow at the cowlick hanging in his eyes. Like Doris, he was a born-and-bred Vermonter with little use for the rest of New England. "Well, anyways, the insurance policy says I'm the one cuts wood, and Pierre when he's up to it, not the paying guests. Nora and Ray got a hard enough time meeting those premiums as it is, what with them getting raised all the time. All they'd need is some kid chopping his toe off with their ax."

Steve forbore to point out that it was the lodge corporation's ax—and for that matter, its insurance premiums too. Again he felt a stir of uneasiness. Just how bad was this money situation, anyway? He set the thought aside for the moment and said impatiently, "Oh, come on, Hal, I'm not gonna hurt myself. My dad says I handle an ax as well as most grown men. It's not a matter of size or age, anyway, unless maybe you're trying to cut down a big tree—it's more a matter of technique."

Hal looked at him thoughtfully. "You're the kid with

the answer to everything, aren't you? I've seen you operate."

"Well, I'm right, aren't I?"

"Maybe so." He grunted, positioning another log on the stump he was using as a chopping block. "Being right don't make you president, though. Sorry, kid, better go find yourself another project."

Steve sat down instead on another stump at the edge of the clearing and put his chin on his hands. He told himself he was perfectly okay, that he was just resting a moment, enjoying the bright, leaf-speckled shade and the pungent pencil-sharpener smell of the cedar shavings. As for finding a project, well, there were plenty of things he could do. In fact, in just a minute he'd go down to the dock and get the red canoe and paddle out into the middle of Heron Lake, away from all these hypercritical, thickheaded, thin-skinned types who seemed to have nothing better to do than pick on him.

But it didn't work. Instead, he found himself replaying what Hal had just said. Never mind president, Steve thought gloomily—right now, with all the people who were mad at him, he wouldn't have a chance of being elected dogcatcher if there'd been such a thing at Potter's Lodge. That reminded him of Motley; he winced and closed his eyes.

Almost the worst part was having Nora so disgusted with him. Steve had always admired the way Nora was so independent and definite about things, seeing whatever needed to be done and doing it quickly, without fuss or apology. He'd thought of himself as being that way too. On the other hand, Nora didn't go around putting other people down, let alone losing her temper and yelling at them when they wouldn't do what she wanted.

Staring between his sneakers at an earwig tunneling under a piece of bark, Steve found himself beginning to doubt his whole happy life up to now. How come he'd never realized before what a rotten person he was?

He thought of what Nora had said about appreciating other people more, their talents and abilities. Talents— that was a laugh. What kind of talent did Angie have, for instance? Of course, there were all those dumb dancing lessons she was always taking at home, tap and ballet and that weird stuff she called modern dance, but who knew if she was even any good at it?

Suddenly Steve sat up straight, feeling the beginnings of a smile tug at the corners of his mouth. Talk about projects, he'd just thought of one that ought to be able to kill at least two birds with a single stone. He'd be doing something nice for Potter's, something everyone would enjoy (at least he hoped they'd enjoy it, and if they didn't, it wouldn't be his fault); and at the same time he'd be showing them all that he wasn't just conceited and self-centered like they thought—that he could take a backseat with the best of them.

Chapter 6

I t won't work," Angie said. She was sprawled in one of the wicker armchairs that graced Cedar Waxwing's living room, still wearing her riding clothes and smelling strongly of horse. "I mean, I think it's a neat idea, but no one will want to be in it if you're going to run it and boss everyone around."

"Then I won't," Steve said humbly. "I'll just help organize things and stay backstage."

"You can still run things from there," Angie told him. "I know you. And what do you mean, 'help organize'? No one else ever gets to organize anything when you're around."

Steve spread his hands helplessly. "Look, Angie, I don't even *want* to run it, particularly—it's not the kind of thing I know anything about." He hesitated, then went on nobly. "We don't even have to say it was my idea. We can say it was yours."

Angie's eyes brightened at this novel prospect, but only for a moment. She sighed and shook her head. "No one would believe that. No, it's better if we just call a meeting and explain about maybe putting on a talent show and how you're not going to be in charge of it, and then—you know—just see what everyone says."

This sounded to Steve like a disastrously unstructured way of proceeding, but he managed not to say so. Angie draped her legs over the side of the chair and began swinging her boots vigorously. She always had trouble thinking unless some part of her body was in motion. "Let's see—all the kids our age, right? Maybe we should make a list."

"Angie, we don't need a list. We know who everyone is." But Steve considered a moment and added reluctantly, "I guess maybe we should invite that Erskine kid too—Fred."

"I didn't meet him yet," Angie said. "He looks quite smart though," she allowed. "Probably he plays the trumpet or something." She laughed suddenly. "Wow, what do you suppose Hugh Curtis will do for his act? Maybe it's not very nice to say, but I can't see him having any talent at all, can you?"

"Everyone does," Steve assured her. It was the article of faith on which he was operating from now on, with all the sincerity he could muster.

In fact, Hugh was the first person to volunteer his skills that evening when the eight of them gathered at Towhee, the small cabin Sally North shared with her father. They'd chosen it as a meeting place because Dr. North was attending the Curtises' slide show down in the rec house, also because Towhee was unusual in having a back porch that faced into the woods—more private, as Steve pointed out. Whether the talent show was actually to be kept secret from the rest of the guests was one of many things they had yet to decide.

"I got this magician kit for my birthday, see," Hugh said eagerly from his perch on the railing, "and I've been practicing a lot. Or I could do juggling. That's another thing I've been working on."

"No juggling," Sally and Angie said in the same breath, then looked away from each other, fighting giggles.

Wanda frowned at them. "Well, I know what I want to do," she announced in her small, precise voice. "Bird calls."

"Bird calls?" Steve stared at her, appalled. Now it was Angie who frowned, and for good measure gave him a hard little punch on the thigh, where Wanda couldn't see.

"I've been learning them from Mrs. Rowan," Wanda explained. "Did you know that each kind of bird has its own special call? And if you copy it, even if you don't do it very well, it'll call you back? Well, actually, some of them have two calls—one just to be friendly, sort of, and the other to sound an alarm."

Only Gus appeared interested in this information; at least he looked up from picking a scab on his knee. Steve grinned, thinking the alarm calls undoubtedly explained

Wanda's sudden interest in birds. Before he could stop himself, he said, "We better find a quiet place to rehearse, then, and keep the windows closed. I mean, we don't want all the birds in the place camped on top of us."

This got a general laugh, he was relieved to see; no one could say he was putting Wanda down, at least not in a mean way. But jeez, bird calls!

"Yes, where *are* we going to rehearse?" Sally asked. "Not here, it's too crowded, and besides, we'd drive my dad crazy."

Everyone started talking at once. From his seat in the only comfortable chair, a rocker in the corner, Fred Erskine held up a pudgy hand for silence. "I think we should decide on the acts first," he said in an authoritative tone.

Rita disagreed. "I need to know how much space we're gonna have." When they all looked at her, she said, "Well, see, I can either yodel or I can do roping tricks. Good thing I brought my lariat along—been keeping it nice and oiled too. But no way I can practice roping on some dinky little porch. Where are we going to do this show, anyway?"

"In the rec house," Steve said promptly. There was a silence, since it was the obvious place and no one was going to be able to think of a better one.

"Too bad there's no curtain there," Fred observed. "Well, probably I can rig up something. Pulleys and so on." Steve eyed him sourly, but everyone else looked impressed. "Wiring, though, that's something else again. You've got your lighting, your microphones—"

"Microphones!" Steve exclaimed. "What do we need microphones for? The rec house isn't exactly Radio City Music Hall, you know."

Angie shot him a warning look, and Gus scowled. "This is supposed to be an open meeting, remember?" he said. "Everyone gets to say whatever they want."

"Right," Fred agreed genially, as if the remark had been addressed to him. He seemed oblivious of the undercurrents among his companions, let alone the fact—unhappily clear enough to Steve—that Gus had come along mainly in the role of watchdog. Fred had been the last to arrive, having spent some time trying to locate Towhee among the cabins on the upper slope, so he hadn't heard the part about Steve's not being in charge. In fact, Steve thought irritably, Fred didn't seem to be aware that Steve was anyone more than just another of the kids. Then he reminded himself that was the way he wanted it, in fact that was the whole point—to prove to everyone he could just vanish into the woodwork and let others enjoy the spotlight.

"I guess I don't need a microphone for my act, anyway," Fred conceded. "Everyone always says it's pretty loud. I'm a one-man band," he explained. "Got my drums and stuff in the back of my brother's van."

Hugh was the only member of the group not struck dumb by this announcement. "What's a one-man band?" he asked wide-eyed, almost toppling off the railing in his excitement. "Wow, it sounds neat!"

While Fred was detailing various pieces of complicated-sounding equipment to him, Steve punched Angie back and whispered, "The trumpet—ha!" Angie shook her head at him and said loudly, "Okay, I know what I'm going to do—some ballet, some modern dance, and tap if I can find my shoes." Angie's method of packing for their two weeks at Potter's was to transfer everything on the floor of her room to her duffel bag. "What about you, Sally?"

Sally was sitting on the top step in the last patch of sunlight filtering down through the trees, her head on her knees. Steve thought maybe she too was trying to shut out the drone of Fred's voice, which had a peculiarly grating quality. On the other hand, she might be thinking of something else entirely. Sally had a way of absenting herself from situations she considered boring or pointless that Steve had always envied, even though he found it maddening when the situation was one of his own devising.

Now she raised her head and said with a yawn, "I hadn't really thought. I know, you'll need someone to hand out programs, won't you? Or I could be a what-d'you-call-it, the person who sits over on the side and hisses—a prompter."

"Sally, we won't need a prompter," Angie told her. "It's not like it's a play, with lines that people have to remember. Anyway, you have to be *in* the show."

"Oh, right. Well, I guess I can do impersonations."

Steve nodded to himself; Sally was a good mimic. The other day she'd done an imitation of Doris waiting on a pair of identical twins—one a vegetarian, one not—that had had his mother and Aunt Marge holding their sides.

"I'll play my harmonica," Gus said, with the air of someone swallowing a pill quickly.

Fred broke off his conversation with Hugh to frown. "A harmonica? That's kind of quiet, isn't it? Well, maybe you could start off the show—you know, right after the curtain goes up and the audience stops talking to see what's gonna happen. And I guess if you had a costume . . . Hey, guys, we need to think about costumes."

Rita said, "Wait a minute. We know what everyone's going to do except Steve."

"Oh, I'll just handle things backstage," he said modestly.

"I don't think that's right," Rita said, and Wanda nodded. "Everybody should be in the show."

"Hey, man, don't worry about backstage," Fred told Steve. "We'll all pitch in, right?" He smiled encouragingly around the circle.

"Well, there's setting up the chairs," Steve said. "And Sally mentioned programs." When everyone just looked at him, he shrugged. "I can't think of anything I can do," he muttered finally. It was no more than the truth, so why should he mind the sardonic little gleam on Gus's face?

"You could recite a poem," Sally suggested, and grinned when he glared at her.

Angie said, "Oh, you'll think of something." She paused, tapping a front tooth with her finger, but nothing seemed to occur to her. Finally she said, "Well, you're good at standing on your head and walking on your hands and stuff like that. Maybe you can work up a tumbling act or something."

Steve swallowed hard. He could just see himself turning somersaults and cartwheels across the rec house floor, and in a costume, yet. What had he gotten himself into, anyway? His whole idea had been to stay out of sight while everyone else did their thing. Maybe he could be the MC. But no, the others would never go for that.

Mercifully, the subject was dropped for now, Fred having decreed it was time they decided on a place to rehearse. After some discussion, it was acknowledged that they couldn't hope to keep the show a secret. Their families would be bound to wonder what was taking up so much of their time during the next few days, and besides, they'd have to clear an hour for the performance in the rec house with Nora and Ray.

Still, they should find an out-of-the-way place for rehearsals, somewhere they could keep the little kids from spying on them. Steve already knew what this place was—the boathouse annex, a good-sized room bare of furniture except for an old couch and some folding beach chairs—but with a heroic effort he refrained from saying so. He sneaked a glance at his watch.

Nine minutes later, after rejecting such possibilities as several temporarily empty cabins (Pine Grosbeak, now that the Erskines had moved to Brown Thrasher, and Nuthatch, being vacated tomorrow by Mr. Jeffries and his nurse in favor of Merganser), the archery range (no cover if it rained, also lots of thistles), and the empty horse stalls at the rear of the stable block (too many doors, and Wanda thought there might be rats in the old straw), someone thought of the boathouse annex. It could even be locked, if they wanted to leave props inside. In fact, it was supposed to be kept locked because of the Sailfish masts and sails that were stored there, only the key seemed to have disappeared.

"No, it hasn't," Steve said. "It's under a rock between the side windows."

It was his one contribution to the discussion.

They agreed to have the first rehearsal the next afternoon, and the meeting broke up to a fusillade of barking from the Kirbys' dog, which had somehow missed their arrival (the Kirbys' cabin was just down the slope from Towhee) but now objected strenuously to their departure.

"Shut up, Motley!" Steve said fiercely as he came around the corner of the cabin. For a moment Motley did, almost as if he might have recognized Steve's voice; then he flung himself against the screen door in a renewed frenzy of yelps and howls.

On the path ahead, Gus cast a disgusted look over his shoulder. "Come on, Steve, he may be a dumb mutt, but he's only trying to be a good watchdog."

"A good watchdog?" Steve said incredulously. "Motley?"

Then he realized Gus didn't know about his session with Motley that morning. The fishing party hadn't returned until almost dinnertime, Gus looking tired and several shades darker from his day on the water, but content with his capture of several large bass. He still wasn't having anything to do with Steve, though. Steve opened his mouth and closed it again as Gus strode away. Whatever he said in Gus's hearing these days had a way of coming out wrong, somehow.

"Say, I've been thinking some more about this dock business," said a voice behind him—Fred Erskine, who else? Steve cursed himself for letting Fred catch up with him. "Actually, the first thing to do would be to fix up the dock over here."

"What's wrong with it?" Steve demanded, turning to glare at him.

"Well, it's pretty dinky, right? I mean, a couple of planks nailed together—you can hardly even call it a dock." Seemingly unfazed by Steve's belligerent manner, Fred gestured expansively at the darkening waters of Heron Lake. "Now, my idea is, you run it a lot farther out into the water—might have to sink some concrete pilings, of course, what with all the mud—and then you can bring some real boats up to it, not just rowboats and canoes. The way the dock is now, see, with the water so shallow, even an outboard motor would probably sink a boat down in the gunk."

"Motors aren't allowed on Heron Lake," Steve was happy to be able to inform him. "I think it might even be a state law."

"Oh." Fred looked thoughtful. "Well, then, about the mud—ever thought of dredging the lake? Like up at the south end," he said, pointing north (and the beavers were at the north end, Steve thought furiously, to say nothing of the herons in the south). "That's what my father did with his lake out in Minnesota—drained the whole thing out and dug a deepwater channel and put down some sand and gravel, and it worked real good. 'Course he had to restock it with fish and stuff afterwards."

Steve stared at him. "Your father owns a lake in Minnesota?" Lakes ran to a fair size out there, or so he'd always heard.

"Used to. He had a vacation home on the big island, and then he added on some guest cottages and a nine-hole golf course on the littler ones. But then when he built the heliport, the wildlife people said he was scaring the game and fish, so finally he sold it—the lake, I mean. That was before I was born, but my brothers told me about it. My dad's sort of a rolling stone, anyway," Fred explained. "Even with business, he gets bored running the same company too long." He named a Fortune 500 company he said his father had just sold. "Mostly we just roam around now, when we're not home in Grosse Pointe or Palm Beach. He and Mom really like it here, though—I guess it sort of reminds them of the Minnesota place, even if it is all rickety and run-down."

"We prefer things rickety," Steve said, but rather weakly. If the Erskines liked Potter's and had that kind of money, maybe he'd better not do anything to rock the boat—such as telling Fred exactly what he thought of all his dumb ideas, for instance.

"Well, been good talking to you," Fred said with an affable nod, and strolled away in the direction of Catbird, his hands in the pockets of his bulky khaki shorts and his striped T-shirt glimmering tigerlike in the dusk.

For a moment Steve found himself wondering what it would be like to be the youngest of a large family—so much the youngest that your oldest brother was almost the age of other kids' fathers and your father himself practically two generations removed from you, more like a grandfather. Then he shrugged. It sure didn't seem to bother Fred much.

Chapter 7

*T*he spell of fine weather began breaking up next day. Clouds jostled the shoulders of the mountains and thunder rumbled fitfully in the distance. By late afternoon, as Steve took the Lake Trail through the woods, the air was heavy and still, the leaves hung limp as wet tissue paper, and the sunlight had a violet tinge that meant a storm was on its way. Even the birds were silent—not so much as an alarm call that Steve could hear.

He and Rita were the last to arrive at the boathouse annex, Rita catching up with him over the last fifty yards with what Steve thought of as her Seven League stride. She carried a new-looking coil of rope over one arm. They crossed the threshold together, then recoiled in mutual dismay. The room was stifling, with a smell so thick you could almost touch it, compounded of varnish, canvas, dust, and stale woodsmoke.

"Whew!" Rita said. "Someone open a window!"

"We just finished closing them," Angie protested.

"Privacy, remember?" Sally said, mopping her dripping face with someone's abandoned beach towel. "And birds."

"Oh, come *on*," Steve began, then fought to control his voice. "I was just kidding about the birds. And as for privacy—well, look for yourself, there's no one else over here, and there won't be, not with a thunderstorm coming. I think it would be safe enough to have the windows open. Of course, I'm not in charge or anything," he made a point of adding.

"Fine with me," Fred said in his cheerful way, and after a moment's hesitation, the others agreed and went to struggle again with the sticky sashes. Opening the windows didn't help the temperature much, but at least the air now smelled of lake water and leaf mold instead of varnish.

"I just hope no one here is scared of thunderstorms," Rita said, looking pointedly at Wanda. Steve could never figure out their relationship. They seemed to be friends, but in a cautious sort of way. Rita seemed to spend almost as much time monitoring Wanda's various anxieties as Wanda herself did in worrying.

Wanda shook her head. "Not here. If lightning strikes, it'll hit that sailboat out there, the one with the metal mast."

Hugh said, "Really?" He peered through the window he'd just opened. "Oh, wow, I love thunderstorms!" Indeed, he looked even more animated than usual, Steve thought, as if the static electricity in the air had somehow found its way into his pores.

Gus said, "Okay, let's get started," and dragged a battered harmonica from his back pocket. "I'm first, right? The sooner we get this rehearsal over with, the less chance of getting soaked on the way back." He took up a position in front of the wide fieldstone fireplace, played a few notes, and stopped. "Maybe you guys should sit down."

"Oh, right." Fred plunked himself in the center of the peeling green plastic couch. "Shove over," Rita told him, and sat down next to him. Wanda and Hugh squeezed in beside her. Angie hunkered down on a sailbag, Sally dusted off a sorry-looking beach chair and climbed into it, and Steve sat on a windowsill, hoping for a breeze. Then they all looked expectantly at Gus.

"This is an Irish song about a soldier who died in battle," he announced, and played a wavery, mournful tune that seemed to go on for a long time. Still, Steve was impressed. The last time he'd heard Gus play the harmonica, he could barely manage the opening bars of "Three Blind Mice." Of course that was when they were about six, he reminded himself, and thought guiltily that it had never occurred to him in all the years since to ask Gus how he was coming along on the harmonica.

The Irish tune was followed by a cowboy lament— Steve thought it was "The Streets of Laredo," but it was sort of hard to tell—and by one verse of "Nobody Knows the Trouble I've Seen," after which Gus made a brief bow, stuck the harmonica back in his pocket, and sat down cross-legged on the rather sooty hearth.

Fred cleared his throat. "Well—" he began, but was interrupted by Rita, who said, "That's it?"

Sally said, "Yes, don't you know any—well, happier songs? Those are all so *sad*."

Gus considered a moment, then shook his head. "That's the kind I like."

"I thought they were very nice," Wanda said quickly, but paused, looking troubled about something. "Don't you ever wipe your harmonica before you put it away?" she asked Gus. "Because of germs, I mean."

He looked perplexed. "Well, but they're just *my* germs. If I loaned it to someone else, sure, I guess I'd wipe it off."

"But you could get your own germs back," Wanda told him. "Like, suppose you had a strep throat when you played your harmonica, and you got better, but next time you played it, the strep germ was still there? I read somewhere that germs like dark little places, like those harmonica holes."

While Gus was objecting that he didn't *have* a strep throat, in fact he felt fine, Fred said, "The problem I see here is the costume. How's he going to be a soldier and a cowboy and a poor black slave, all at the same time?" But instantly he answered his own question. "I know—hats."

"Hats?" Angie echoed.

"Sure. A soldier hat, see, and a cowboy hat—"

"Oh, I get it. Right—Gus can borrow your cowboy

hat, can't he, Rita? I don't know where we'd get a soldier hat, though." Angie knitted her brow, ignoring Rita's objection that she never loaned anyone her Stetson, and anyway planned to wear it herself for her roping act. "Let's see, I guess for the slave he could wear one of those big, floppy straw hats . . ."

"My aunt has a hat like that," Hugh volunteered, waving his hand in the air as if he thought he was in a classroom. "You know, the one she wears when she helps Nora in the garden." Mrs. Curtis was a stout, slow-moving lady who occasionally bestirred herself to cut a few flowers for the dining room; mostly she spent her time playing bridge and going for leisurely country drives with her equally stodgy husband.

Steve, on his windowsill, was torn between mirth at the thought of Gus in Mrs. Curtis's straw hat (trimmed with plastic daisies, as he recalled) and despair at the pace of the rehearsal. At this rate, they'd be lucky to make it back to the lodge in time for dinner, which tonight featured corn on the cob and Terence's secret-formula fried chicken. Luckily, a flare of lightning and a bone-jarring clap of thunder got everyone's attention, and he was able to say mildly into the pause, "Who's next?"

Everyone agreed the second act on the program should be something livelier and also more upbeat, as Fred put it. Rita thought this made her roping exhibition the logical choice, but Fred said they shouldn't repeat the cowboy theme so soon (cowboy theme? Steve thought a little wildly—a hat and a tune most people probably wouldn't even recognize?), so Angie was chosen instead. Only now did it occur to Angie that she was going to need music to dance to. There was the old record player in the rec house that Ray used for square dances, but no one remembered seeing anything but rock and country music and kiddie albums among the dusty pile of records there. Wanda said her father probably wouldn't mind playing the piano for Angie if she could find the right kind of sheet music in the piano bench. Or she could ask Mr. Kirby, who knew how to play by ear.

Steve could see Angie trying to picture Mr. Kirby in the accommodating role of her dance accompanist. Finally she said she'd decide later. For now, she'd just do a few steps so they could get an idea of her act. "I need to figure out about my costume, though," she said, executing a rapid series of slightly off-balance pirouettes that almost knocked Steve off his windowsill. "I mean, you can wear any old thing for modern dance and tap"—here she bounced down into a split and up again—"but for ballet you need to look *right*." She tried a few tap steps, explaining they'd work better when she found her tap shoes. "Maybe I could tack some material on my bathing suit for a skirt—you know, something sort of ruffly."

"How about the bathroom curtains?" Steve suggested, thinking of the strips of netting that adorned the window of Cedar Waxwing's single bathroom. Well, they had ruffles, didn't they?—even if they were also a rather peculiar shade of pistachio green. Angie gave him an injured look and flounced back down onto her sailbag. Several people applauded.

Sally said she thought she should come next on the program, since there hadn't been any talking so far, only she hadn't decided yet whom to impersonate—she'd surprise them next time. Rita pointed out there weren't going to be all that many rehearsals, and Fred said, yes, couldn't she at least give them a sample?

"Do Princess Di at the polo match," Steve urged, and ducked his head as everyone turned to look at him. "Well, it's funny," he said defensively.

Sally obliged from her near-reclining position in the low beach chair. Somehow, with just a flip of her hair and a demure lowering of her eyelids, she transformed herself into Princess Diana watching Prince Charles gallop up and down a polo field—or rather pretending to watch, since at the same time she was talking out of the side of her mouth to the person next to her, mostly about clothes. "A simply smashing little afternoon dress, and with the royal discount, it'll cost the Exchequer only two million pounds." Sally even did a pretty good English accent. She got to travel a lot with her father when he went to medical conventions.

"Okay, celebrity imitations," Fred said as the laughter died down, with the air of someone ticking off a mental list.

Steve opened his mouth to say something and closed it again. Outside, the rain had begun—fat, splashy drops that thinned quickly into a steady downpour. Steve found himself peering through the blur for the sailboat Wanda had mentioned earlier, but he could see nothing but gray lake water. Probably it had put in to shore in plenty of time. No need to assume, as Wanda undoubtedly would (luckily she seemed to have forgotten about it), that the boat had capsized and gone down with all hands, including babies and old people in wheelchairs. Anyway, the storm seemed to be moving on, the sky already growing lighter beyond the curtain of rain.

Meanwhile the program called for action again. Rita planted herself in the middle of the room, loosened the coil of her lariat, and began whirling the noose over her head. As it gained speed, the rope gave off a nasty hiss. "I like to start with figure eights," she explained while the group on the couch scrunched down and the others scrambled out of the way to flatten themselves against the walls. "Only sometimes it takes a while to get them going. Also this ceiling is kind of low."

Proof of this fact arrived a few seconds later, when Rita achieved a figure eight whose upper loop managed to snag the blade of a heavy wooden oar stored up on the rafters.

"Watch it!" Steve yelled, and bounded off his windowsill in time to catch the oar before it decapitated Hugh and Wanda.

"Maybe you should do the rest outdoors," Angie said nervously.

"In the rain?" Rita looked indignant, though Steve thought cowboys never let a little rain bother them when they were out slinging their lariats around. "Anyway, that was just warm-up stuff. What I really do is rope something—you know, lasso it."

She looked around the room for something to lasso. Nothing seemed to be the right size or shape. Fred suggested she try roping a person, but no one offered to play this role (including Fred himself, Steve noticed). "I know—volunteers from the audience," Fred decided, and sat back, looking pleased with himself. "Always a good idea to involve your audience."

"Or she could lasso the piano," Gus said. Everyone looked to see if he was joking, but he didn't seem to be. "Well, it's a big target," he explained. "And it's heavy, so she couldn't tip it over."

"Interesting thought, anyway," Fred said kindly, and Gus scowled. Steve was pleased to see that Fred was beginning to get on Gus's nerves almost as badly as he did on Steve's. On the other hand, maybe he'd better tell Gus about the Erskines being rich. If Gus got mad enough, even Fred might notice; it might actually dawn on him that he wasn't quite as welcome at Potter's as he seemed to think he was. And if Fred was unhappy here, who knew if his family would even stay through the week they'd signed up for, let alone supply the money the lodge might need to keep going?

Pondering all this, Steve only half heard Sally asking him what he'd decided to do for his act. He raised his head to find everyone looking at him.

"Oh, I've got a few ideas," he said carelessly, "but they still need work. I'll have something ready by the next rehearsal, for sure."

Hugh said anxiously, "Hey, what about me? I haven't done my act yet."

"Neither has Wanda," Rita pointed out.

Wanda said quickly, "Oh, I don't really need to do mine for rehearsal. I mean, I know it's kind of specialized, and probably only a few people will be interested." Everyone hastened to assure her this wasn't true, that they were all eager to hear her bird noises, and finally she was persuaded to stand up and produce several nervous whistles, with long pauses in between to compose herself and (as she put it) think herself into the bird's head.

"Yeah," Fred said, "maybe you could sort of act out being the different birds? Or, I don't know, do something with feathers?"

Wanda stared at him; finally she shook her head. "I don't think so," she said. "Okay, here's my last one." Scrunching her narrow shoulders and thrusting her neck forward in a way that actually *was* sort of birdlike, now Steve thought about it, she uttered a series of piercing notes that sounded like someone whistling to his dog. In spite of himself, Steve was gratified to recognize this call as belonging to a cardinal, one of the few birds he could identify.

Wanda sat down. Hugh began rummaging through a large black case full of colored scarves and oddly shaped containers with visibly false bottoms.

Gus looked over at Steve and said, "What time is it?" Steve was the only one wearing a watch besides Fred.

"Almost five."

"Oh. I thought it was later."

"So did I."

It was the closest Steve had felt to Gus in several days.

"Okay, everyone, I'm ready," Hugh announced, springing to his feet and clapping a black magician's hat on his head. "We'll begin with a few simple card tricks," he said with an ingratiating, toothy grin (probably the manual told him to smile, Steve thought), and fanned out a pack of cards. "Now I need someone from the audience to come forward and pick a card, any card."

Unfortunately the hat was the collapsible kind, and Hugh hadn't straightened it out all the way. Before anyone could respond to his summons, it fell down around his ears. In clutching at it, he dropped the pack of cards.

"Oh, good, Fifty-Two Pickup," Sally said, joining the others on her hands and knees. "My favorite game."

Hugh said nervously, "Just don't look at the cards when you pick them up, okay? There's some special stuff you're not supposed to see."

Steve suppressed a groan. Scooping up an ace of hearts that felt suspiciously thin and slippery, he got a splinter in the heel of his hand, opened his mouth to curse, and suppressed that too.

The rain had stopped by the time they trooped back through the dripping woods, avoiding the muddy center of the trail, though thunder still muttered in the distance. As Steve came down into the yard between the car shed and the old frame house that served as a staff dormitory, he realized he was also hearing raised voices from the rear of the lodge. In no hurry to listen to Angie on the subject of the bathroom curtains once they got back to Cedar Waxwing, he edged onto the end of the kitchen porch, where he couldn't be seen from the windows. One of the voices was Mrs. Kirby's.

"I'm terribly sorry!" she was exclaiming in distraught tones. "I simply can't imagine what got into him. Except for the storm, of course—he's terrified of thunder and lightning, poor thing."

A voice Steve recognized as Terence's—Terence at his most fiery and redheaded—said, "Poor thing, my eye," only that wasn't quite what he said. "Two drumsticks and a wing, and batter all over the floor! To say nothing of what he did to Doris."

"Now, now"—this was Ray's soothing bass—"Doris is perfectly all right, or will be when she stops crying and changes into a fresh uniform. I'm sure Motley didn't mean to knock her down. He was just overexcited, and probably they both slipped on the batter."

"Overexcited! Out of control is more like it. In fact *amok* is what I'd call it—a great filthy dog running amok in my kitchen. Well, I won't have it, Ray. I'll manage dinner tonight somehow, but unless that creature is over the state line by tomorrow morning, I'm outta here."

"I think it's elephants that run amok," Mrs. Kirby objected. "And Motley's perfectly clean, we gave him a flea bath only last week—"

Ray interrupted, evidently drawing her aside, and a

low-voiced conversation ensued, punctuated by the sound of Terence bashing pots and pans around. Steve knew that Ray lived in dread of having Terence quit on him in the middle of a season, though he accepted the fact that once Terence finished his training, he would undoubtedly wind up plying his trade in far more exalted precincts than the kitchen of Potter's Lodge. Meanwhile, the other fact that Terence was an ardent fisherman, almost as nutty about fly casting as Gus, continued to draw him back each summer.

It occurred to Steve that he was eavesdropping, and that if Ray caught him at it, he'd be in big trouble again. Still, there was nothing wrong with taking a shortcut through the kitchen yard to the beginning of the cabin path—people did it all the time.

He was just opposite the back door when it swung open and Mrs. Kirby edged out, saying in a subdued voice, "Yes, I understand—though calling it the last straw does seem a bit— But of course we'll do our very best. You know how we love it here, Ray, such utter peace and beauty, we always feel restored after our two weeks." Ray said something Steve couldn't hear. "Well, naturally they do, and if Motley's been *disturbing* people somehow . . ."

The screen door clapped shut. Steve had made a pretense of moving on, but wasn't surprised when Mrs. Kirby caught up with him and said urgently, "Oh, Steve, may I talk to you for a moment?"

Taking his elbow, she steered him around the corner

of the lodge and down the slope to the circular flowerbed beside the driveway. The flag still hung wet and limp on its pole, but hollyhocks and delphinium glistened freshly in a shaft of sunlight piercing the clouds.

With a glance around to make sure no one was within earshot, Mrs. Kirby cleared her throat and said, "I'm afraid we've been given a sort of ultimatum about Motley. About—well, disciplining him." She gave Steve a stern look. "I don't mean *really* disciplining him, of course, but . . . well, just getting him to the point where he'll listen when people say 'no' to him. And maybe it would be good if he could learn 'stay' too, when people tell him to."

Steve nodded, keeping his face impassive, though he was grinning inside.

"The thing is"—she bit her lip, looking down at the border of frilly white petunias—"I'm just no good at making Motley behave. Somehow it *pains* me to have to make him do anything he doesn't want to do. Or stop him doing something he does want to do. Even when I try, I think he knows I don't really mean it. And my husband's even worse than I am—he's a complete softie where Motley's concerned." She sighed, then gave Steve a bright little smile of appeal. "So, anyway, I wondered if you'd be willing to work with him. You know, have regular training sessions, like the one you had yesterday. I can tell Motley likes you, so I don't think he'd mind too much, and—well, I think if Ray realized we were making a genuine effort . . ."

Steve waited a beat, enjoying her discomfiture, and then said with a shrug, "Sure, I don't mind. But I'd have to make a couple of conditions."

"Anything," Mrs. Kirby said quickly.

"First, I need a box of dog biscuits. Dog biscuits won't spoil him," he told her firmly, "and they'll be good for his teeth. Second, I want to be able to take Motley off by himself, with no one around to distract him."

"Like me, you mean." She smiled ruefully, and Steve found himself smiling back. "It's a deal. I just hope he won't give you too much trouble. And please don't feel you have to bother with fancy things like 'heel' and 'sit' and 'lie down.' I mean, we don't expect *miracles*."

Why am I smiling? Steve thought as Mrs. Kirby gave his shoulder a grateful parting squeeze and strode away, looking self-possessed and confident once more. Just getting Motley to accept the word *no* was going to be a small miracle in itself.

Chapter 8

*F*or a while the next day, it looked as though there might never be another rehearsal of the talent show. Partly this was because of the tennis tournament, which was still meandering along in its casual way. Wanda, Hugh, and Sally were still in it, though if Sally and her father lost once more, they wouldn't make the semifinals. Mostly, though, it was because of Fred Erskine. Wanda had taken exception to Fred's manner at the first rehearsal, Rita was appalled by a suggestion he'd tossed out for turning the lower part of the Ledge Trail into a skateboard run, Sally thought he was a bore, and Angie was annoyed because he expected her to chase down things like curtain wire and soldier hats that had been his own idea in the first place. Even Hugh thought he talked too much and was beginning to wonder if Fred as a one-man band might not be too much of a good thing.

As for Gus, he was furious at some remarks Fred had

made about Pierre. "He called him an old geezer, right where Pierre could've heard!"

"Well, Pierre's English isn't too good," Steve pointed out. "He might not know what it meant."

"He was scything down some tall grass behind the little kids' playground," Gus continued, glowering at Steve, "going slow like he does, but getting it *done*, you know? And Fred said, 'Who is that old geezer, anyway?' and then a lot of stuff about how he ought to be pensioned off, anyone could see we needed a really able-bodied man for all the work that needs doing around here. Also what if there was an emergency and Pierre wouldn't understand unless you yelled at him in French? A lot he knows. Pierre is the—the soul of this place!"

"Well, the Erskines are new this year," Steve said cautiously. "I mean, Fred probably hasn't had a chance to talk to Pierre yet." Not that Pierre himself ever said much of anything, he qualified to himself. Still, he knew what Gus meant about Pierre. It had something to do with his smile and the clear northern blue of his eyes, maybe also with the way he moved—easy and soft-footed in spite of his age, with a jaunty set to his wiry shoulders.

Gus was staring at Steve. "Come on, you can't *like* the guy! The rest of the family's okay, I guess, except for that hotshot brother who's always showing off his muscles, but Fred . . . Fred's a jerk!"

Steve shrugged, looking away. "I'm just saying maybe

we should give him a little more time. You know, not get down on him too soon."

For the second or third time, he was on the verge of telling Gus about Potter's financial plight and how crucial the Erskines' support might be, but found himself hesitating once again. He didn't have any hard facts yet, after all, and Steve disliked presenting a case unless he was absolutely sure of it. Anyway, it was too late now; Gus was already stalking away in disgust, presenting Steve with what had become the all-too-familiar view of his back.

Finally, though, there was an emergency meeting about the talent show in the middle of Heron Lake—not one that anyone planned, one that just happened. Steve and Angie were out in the red canoe, practicing for the two-man phase of next week's canoe race, when they spotted two rowboats on a collision course. One contained Gus and Sally, who was sculling very slowly and delicately (the only kind of rowing she liked) so that Gus could troll. The other boat was being propelled jerkily across the water by Hugh Curtis, with Wanda and Rita in the stern. Hugh, of course, never looked over his shoulder when he rowed, and Wanda was less alert than usual, being intent on arranging something in the large glass terrarium she held in her lap.

Steve gave a shout, and he and Angie sped across the water to intercept them. It was a near thing, with Hugh almost knocking Rita overboard in a panicky (and unnecessary) effort to ship his oars as the canoe cut toward him.

"Well, here we all are," Sally observed, once all three boats were rocking safely nose to nose. "Except Fred, come to think of it." No one had seen Fred do anything more venturesome than wade into Great Harriman as far as his waist, remark on how cold the water was, and wade out again. "Are we having a rehearsal today, or what? I've been trying to figure out how to do Madonna, but I don't want to bother if we're never going to do the show."

There was a bemused silence, broken only by a faint lapping of water.

Rita said, "What I think is, we need is someone to be the head of it—someone that's not Fred. I don't mean a *boss*," she explained quickly, while everyone made a point of not looking at Steve. "Just a person who'll be the one to decide things like when the rehearsals are and who should come next on the program and stuff like that."

"Like a director," Wanda said with a nod, as if she'd already given this some thought.

"I'll do it!" Hugh said, waving his hand in the air and disturbing a cloud of midges that had settled around his head. When no one rushed to take him up on this offer, he said, "Well, gosh, we *gotta* have the show."

"You have a lot of practicing to do, though, Hugh," Angie said. "Like, it should be someone who already has his act together." Steve saw her hear how this sounded. "If you know what I mean," she added lamely.

"Also someone who's not in the tennis tournament," Rita put in.

"Also someone *calm*," Sally finished, not unkindly.

"Like Gus," said Wanda, gazing into her terrarium as if it were a crystal ball.

"Gus?" Steve said, startled.

Gus shot him a belligerent look, though Steve hadn't meant to express anything more than surprise at this unexpected suggestion. The others too were looking a bit doubtful—even Wanda had gone a little pink, as if she wished she hadn't spoken—but Gus didn't seem to notice. "I don't mind," he said with a shrug. "Anything would be better than all this futzing around."

He paused, evidently to consult an inner calendar, and went on briskly. "Okay, we'll have the next rehearsal tomorrow morning—ten o'clock sharp, and nobody be late. It's already too complicated to figure out a time for today. If anyone's supposed to go riding or play tennis or go for a hike in the morning, they'll just have to change it." He picked up his rod, looking satisfied with these arrangements, and added, with a gleam that Steve thought explained his willingness to assume this new responsibility, "Somebody better tell Fred."

Tomorrow at ten was when Steve had planned to work with Motley, as he had today, but he didn't want to say so. As far as anyone else was concerned, he was just taking Motley for long, invigorating walks along the back road to Gilead. Maybe he could fit in another session tonight before the square dance, though it was quite a distance to the abandoned logging trail he'd chosen as a training ground. Of course, that was why he'd chosen it—not only did the trail end in a convenient clearing deep in the woods, just getting there was an efficient way of tiring Motley out.

Up to now, Steve hadn't paid much attention to Todd Erskine, Fred's college-age brother with the adoring girlfriend. Indeed, his contact with the rest of the Erskines had been limited to friendly nods from the married brothers and their wives and an exchange about the weather with Mr. Erskine, who'd observed that there was nothing like a thunderstorm to clear the air. Since they were skirting an enormous puddle in the road at the time, on their way back from dinner, Steve wondered if Mr. Erskine was going to say something about improving the drainage or maybe even paving the road over. But he didn't; he just gazed through the reeds at the sunset clouds reflected in Heron Lake and strolled on with a contented smile on his large face.

In the morning, though, he saw what Gus meant about Todd. Rehearsal was just under way in the boathouse annex when he came in for a Sailfish mast— or barged in, rather, shoving the door open without bothering to knock, although it must have been clear from the closed windows and the strains of loud, if tinny, music from Angie's transistor that something was going on inside.

"This where they keep the sailing gear?" he demanded of no one in particular, brushing past Angie in mid-arabesque.

"Oh, hey, Todd, you taking a boat out?" Fred said eagerly, actually getting to his feet to turn down the radio.

"Yeah, thought we'd go for a little spin. Jan's never been sailing before, isn't that wild?" Jan was the girlfriend, waiting down by the beach in her yellow bikini—Steve could see her through the open door, talking to one of the teenage waitresses, her coppery hair rippling in the breeze. It was a bright, cool day with an edge of fall in the air. "Give me a hand, willya, kid?"

This was addressed to Hugh, who merely gaped at him. Steve picked up one end of a mast that was lying against the wall and helped Todd jockey it around toward the door. "Lake sailing can be kind of tricky," Steve offered, checking the furl of the sail.

"So?" Todd favored him with a cool stare.

"I just mean you've gotta watch the wind, the way it swirls around sometimes. People are always capsizing."

"Good thing we know how to swim, then, right?" Todd flexed his broad shoulders and grinned at the others, showing oversized, square white teeth; everything about him was oversized, Steve thought, including his loud voice. "I doubt this nice little breeze is going to give us any trouble," he told Steve condescendingly, "but thanks for the warning, pal."

Steve was aware of everyone scowling at him, including Gus, but he persisted. "Keep your eye on the notch between Harriman Mountain and Buckle Peak," he advised from the doorway as Todd shouldered the mast and started off across the picnic area. "At the head of the lake, over on the left. That's where the big gusts usually come from, and sometimes you can see them ruffling the water."

"Oh, come on, Steve, I'm losing my music," Angie complained, fiddling with the transistor dial as the lone classical music station in the area squawked and faded. (The radio was a temporary expedient, to be replaced by Nora's tape deck as soon as Angie remembered to ask if she could borrow it; she'd decided against complicating her act with a human accompanist.)

Fred said, "Yeah, you don't have to worry about my brother handling himself on the water, for Pete's sake. He's on his college swim team, besides being practically a championship water-skier. Also he goes sailing a lot with friends," he added, forestalling Steve's question. "Crewing, or whatever it's called. 'Course he's used to bigger boats."

Watching through the window as Todd launched the Sailfish and motioned Jan aboard, Steve thought that fact alone might present a problem. Did Todd know about the centerboard? He hadn't made any move to put it down, as far as Steve could see. Well, maybe he was waiting to get farther out in the lake. While Angie went through the rest of her routine—a tortuous process, since she couldn't seem to find any music on the radio that was right for tap dancing—Steve continued to keep an eye on the diminishing white triangle of the sail.

"Steve, do you *mind?*" Sally's voice recalled him to the rehearsal midway through her impersonation of Cher, who she'd decided would be easier to do than

Madonna. She was eyeing him angrily, one hand on her hip—looking more like Cher, in fact, than she'd managed to do so far. "I know it's not very good yet, but you don't have to turn your back on me."

"Sorry," Steve said. "I was just checking on Fred's brother."

Angie giggled. "You're getting to be almost as much of a worrywart as Wanda. Sorry," she added to Wanda, who said mildly, "That's okay."

Annoyed, Steve said, "I'm almost sure he never put the centerboard down."

"Almost sure?" Gus said sarcastically. "Wow, that's a switch."

"He could be in real trouble if he didn't," Steve pointed out. "Not so much capsizing, I guess, if the wind stays light, but drifting."

"Well, that's his problem," Gus told him, looking impatient. "Okay, Sally, I guess you don't need to do any more. Rita, you're up next."

But Rita had joined Steve at the window. "Which boat is it?" she asked.

There were quite a few white sails in the middle of the lake now. Steve stared hard, then shook his head. "I can't tell anymore."

From the other lakefront window, Wanda—always ready to share someone else's worry—asked Hugh if he'd brought his binoculars along, but he hadn't. Fred got up and looked over her shoulder. "I don't see any boat that looks like it's in trouble," he said dismissively.

"Anyway, if there was a problem with the what-d'you-call-it, Todd would have figured it out by now."

"Can we please get on with the rehearsal?" Gus demanded.

Steve glared at Fred as the latter returned to his seat on the couch. "Centerboard," he said loudly. "It's instead of a keel. If you don't have a keel, you can't control the boat, and if you can't control the boat—"

He checked himself, remembering it was in everyone's best interests to keep Fred happy. "Okay, okay," he said, raising a hand, "your brother can handle himself on the water. Never mind. Sorry I said anything." He plunked himself back down on the windowsill. "What's Rita gonna catch with her rope today—another oar, or maybe that big old fire extinguisher in the corner? Maybe she should stick to yodeling instead."

He was instantly sorry for his tone, if not his words. Everyone was glowering at him. Rita said with dignity, "I'm just going to do some loops and jumps today—that's where I make big circles and jump through them. I'm working on the roping part with Karen. She said she'd be my volunteer." Karen was the college girl who took care of the horses. "As for yodeling, I might even add that to my act if I can figure out a place to practice it. My aunt hates the sound, she says it sounds like a sick cat. But anyway, you're a big one to talk. I bet you don't even have an act yet."

"As a matter of fact, I do," Steve said recklessly, though the only idea that had occurred to him thus far was so crazy he'd been resisting even thinking about it. "Only it's not ready yet. It probably won't be ready until the dress rehearsal."

"Dress rehearsal," Angie repeated, running a hand distractedly through her hair. "Oh, gosh, and we still haven't organized about costumes and lights and a curtain and everything. . . ." She looked back at Steve. "Aren't you going to tell us what it is? Your act?"

"No," Steve said.

"Oh, who cares what it is," Gus said, losing his temper. "He can play 'Chopsticks' on the piano for all I care. Look, you guys ever want to get out of here? Because it's a really nice day outside, in case you haven't noticed, and I for one have had it with being cooped up in here."

Indeed, Gus's main idea as director seemed to be to get them through the rehearsal as rapidly as possible. Angie said as much to Steve when it finally came to an end, climaxed by Fred's performance of "Stars and Stripes Forever" on the few instruments in his band portable enough to carry through the woods—a kazoo, a tambourine, and a cowbell.

"Gus isn't even trying to *help*," she complained. "Like telling Hugh not to keep looking things up in his magician's book every two seconds, and getting Wanda to stop standing on tiptoe and twitching her eyebrows in that weird way she's been doing. And he still lets Fred talk whenever he feels like it. All Gus does is not listen."

She kicked moodily at a clump of black-eyed Susans beside the door. "Maybe he thinks the show is going to be so awful anyway, it's not worth trying to fix it." When Steve was silent, she flared at him. "I bet that's what you think too, the way you just sit there and never even make a suggestion." Before Steve could object that he'd practically been forbidden to make suggestions, she added with a logic that seemed skewed even for Angie, "No wonder you didn't want anyone to know the show was your idea!" and marched away.

Steve waited until the others had collected their gear and departed. Then he went around behind the annex and down onto the rocks by the boat slip. The breeze had freshened; most of the white sails were tilted over now against the blue water as the boats sliced along on their assorted tacks.

But one boat in the near distance, sure enough, was behaving peculiarly, not moving forward so much as skidding sideways. Shading his eyes, Steve made out the burly figure of Todd Erskine beside the mast. He did something to the sail, then moved back to the tiller. Now instead of skidding, the boat sat dead in the water, the sail flapping. Todd yanked the tiller back and forth, to no avail. Something about the way he did all this suggested it was a sequence that had been repeating itself for some time.

Steve remembered seeing an old megaphone in the annex. Probably if he just yelled "Centerboard!" through it as loudly as he could, Todd would get the idea and release the catch. On the other hand, there were a lot of people at the swimming area on this sunny morning, sunbathing or splashing in the water or diving from the raft, and more would be arriving soon with their picnic lunches. Steve didn't have much use for Todd, what he'd seen of him anyway, but maybe he should try not to embarrass him in front of an audience, if only because Todd was an Erskine.

Maybe, too, it would be just as well not to advertise the fact that he, Steve, had foreseen exactly the sort of trouble Todd had gotten himself into. Given the enormous, gut-wrenching effort he'd been making lately not to be too sure or too right about anything, it would be a shame to spoil it now.

He thought of the day he'd taken his truant swim, and how Ray had rowed out to speak to him instead of just bellowing from the shore. Of course that was more because of the Erskines than to spare Steve's feelings, but still . . .

Resignedly, Steve upended one of the smaller rowboats, found the oars lying under it, shoved its stern into the water, and clambered in. He rowed out into the lake, doing his best to look casual, as if he were just getting some exercise, without any particular destination in mind. Even when he was close enough to the Sailfish to yell in a normal kind of yelling voice, he refrained from doing so. Todd had reset the sail and managed to catch some wind again, with the result that the boat had gone back into its sideways skid. He jiggled the tiller angrily, but the bow didn't respond. Jan was no longer draped gracefully across the bow, Steve saw, but sat huddled beside the mast, looking forlorn and goose-pimply in her yellow bikini.

Steve waited until he was almost alongside, keeping to windward so the Sailfish wouldn't drift into him, and then said in a conversational tone, "I think maybe you need to put the centerboard down."

Todd jerked his head around. This time his stare was a good deal less insolent. But Steve had to give him full marks for a quick recovery. "Oh, right," he said. "Didn't think I'd bother, a light breeze like this one, but probably she'll handle better with it down."

He looked between his feet where Steve was pointing and released the catch. There was a clunk as the heavy board bit down into the water. Immediately the boat heeled over, almost spilling Jan off the bow. "Head up into the wind!" Steve called as she clutched at the mast. Todd hauled at the sail, now heavy and stiff with the full weight of the breeze, but pushed the tiller the wrong way. There was a precarious moment when Steve was sure they were going over; but somehow the maneuver resolved itself into a lucky jibe.

"Guess I'm more used to a wheel than a tiller," Todd mumbled, red-faced, and added something about the directions being reversed that Steve didn't quite catch—the sailboat was already swishing away on its new course.

Steve picked up his oars and rowed after it, still trying to look casual. Since the Sailfish happened to be heading toward shore, aimed in the general direction of the boathouse, he wasn't too surprised to hear Todd tell Jan he thought they might as well take her back in now. Steve could only hope he wouldn't try to return the boat to the beach, a process that would involve at least two or three tacks back up along the shoreline.

But maybe Todd, too, was conscious of the populated swimming area. He settled for a rough landing offshore, dropping the sail safely short of the rocks and paddling in the rest of the way. Steve watched to make sure he pulled the centerboard back up—actually, he didn't need to watch, he would have heard the horrible grinding sound it made, scraping against the rock—and then took a few more turns with the oars to complete his self-portrait as a mere idler in a rowboat.

By the time he'd beached the rowboat and gone around the annex, Todd was nowhere in sight. Jan was standing down on the ledge, combing the snarls from her long hair and talking to his mother and Aunt Marge, ensconced with their books and crossword puzzles and suntan lotion in two of the big slant-back wooden armchairs. Jan caught sight of Steve and waved merrily.

"Thank goodness for your son," she was saying as Steve approached. "We were having a terrible time out there—Todd simply *couldn't* figure out what was wrong with the boat."

Steve stared at her in disbelief. The stupid girl didn't even know enough about sailing to realize she should keep her mouth shut. Todd would probably kill her. Steve himself wouldn't have minded wiping the grateful smile from her face.

"Did you bring my lunch over, Mom?" he asked quickly, hoping to forestall any more details.

"Of course, as soon as he mentioned the centerboard thing—"

"I'm starved," Steve interrupted, falling on the knapsack beside his mother's chair like a man just released from a year's diet of bread and water; but the damage was done. Andrew Munson was standing nearby, wrapped in a beach towel, all wide eyes and flapping ears. Soon his mouth would be flapping too, Steve knew from experience. It wasn't only that Andrew was a natural gossip; for some reason, he was also an admirer of Steve's.

Steve's mother was studying him quizzically. That morning she'd asked him if he was feeling all right, he'd seemed so subdued lately.

"Gosh, that looks good," Jan said as Steve tore the waxed paper from his egg sandwich and rummaged around for the pickles. "Are those homemade cookies? You must have a bigger oven in your cabin than we do—ours is a dinky little thing."

"This is just the camp lunch," Mrs. Hyatt said, looking puzzled. "We aren't in a housekeeping cabin, and in any case, baking peanut-butter cookies is hardly my idea of a vacation."

"Especially since you always burn them," said Aunt Marge, who was the better cook.

Jan exclaimed, "The camp makes picnic lunches? Oh, how great! We thought you either had to eat in the dining room or fix your own. Wait'll I tell Mrs. Erskine—she's been spending half the morning making sandwiches."

"The forms are in the desk drawer," Steve told her crossly, bearing his lunch away to one of the picnic tables.

Andrew followed him. "Wow!" he said. "Did you have to go out on the lake and *rescue* someone?"

Chapter 9

What's he doing here?" Rita demanded as Steve led Motley into the rec house.

"Yeah," Gus said, "that's all we need, a dog fouling up the dress rehearsal. Come on, Steve, get him out of here."

"I can't," Steve told him, tying Motley's leash to one leg of the Ping-Pong table. "He's my act. Sit, Motley."

Motley sat. After a moment, with an apologetic look at Steve—who after all hadn't issued the command—he lay down and rested his nose on his paws.

The others were momentarily speechless.

"But you can't!" Angie was the first to find her voice. "A *dog*? What are you going to do with him? He doesn't even know how to behave!"

"Yes, he does," Steve said. "I've been training him. He can't do anything fancy yet, just simple tricks, but anyway, that's my act."

"Simple tricks, like Hugh's?" Sally grimaced, but then added thoughtfully, "As a matter of fact, he hasn't been barking as much lately. Or at least when he does bark and Mrs. Kirby tells him no, sometimes he stops."

"Ugly-looking mutt," was Fred's comment. "Might have some terrier blood, I suppose," he conceded, peering around his battery of drums for a better look at Motley. "They're the best kind for doing tricks— terriers, and those little poodles. You know, the ones you see at the circus, jumping through hoops and riding on horses' backs and—"

"He has a name, you know," Steve interrupted coldly. "Motley."

Motley beat his tail against the floor.

Gus was looking interested rather than impatient, for a change. "You try teaching him to swim yet?" he asked.

"Nope," Steve said, and added with a straight face, "Just to sail."

It was a poor choice of joke, as he realized belatedly when no one laughed or even smiled. They all thought he was referring to his so-called rescue of Todd Erskine and his girlfriend—who, incidentally, were barely speaking to each other these days.

The only good thing to have come out of that whole episode, Steve thought bleakly, was that the Erskines were now devouring picnic lunches as fast as the kitchen could turn them out. Nora had been apologetic when Steve explained. "It was my fault for forgetting to tell them in the first place," she said. "I thought they were just economizing by making their own sandwiches."

When Steve said he didn't think they need to economize, she nodded—so at least she knew about the Erskines being rich, he thought—but said obscurely, "The ones who don't need to are often the ones who do."

"Okay, let's get going," Gus was saying, dodging a bed sheet Angie and Rita were trying to drape over a long, sagging wire strung across the front of the room. "Is everyone here? Where's Wanda?"

"Here I am." Wanda appeared in the doorway in her tennis clothes, looking pleased to have had her absence noted. She laid her racket carefully across a chair and blotted her sweaty face with one of the two hand towels she carried in her tote bag whenever she played tennis—a regular dry towel and a soggy, wet one in a plastic bag, to apply in the event of sunstroke or heat prostration. "We won," she told Hugh, who was busy gluing tiny mirrors inside the cuffs and lapels of a sleazy-looking black jacket that had come with his magician's kit. "So I guess we'll be playing you and Mrs. Kirby again, only this time it'll be the finals."

She turned her head and quailed—not at Motley, as Steve first thought, but at the sight of the rifle Gus was in the act of slinging over his shoulder. "What's that for?" she said, her gaze darting around the room as if she expected to see armed bandits lurking in the corners.

"We couldn't find a soldier hat," Gus explained sourly. "No way I'm gonna wear some dumb cardboard thing Angie said she'd make, so I borrowed a gun from Hal. It's not loaded," he added, trying to adjust the strap so the butt of the rifle wouldn't bang against the back of his knee.

"Oh." Wanda looked as if she thought they ought to double-check this, but seemed to think better of saying so. "I brought something for my costume too. Well, I couldn't find enough feathers to make anything with," she told Fred defensively, "even with Andrew helping me look. You think there are lots of feathers around, but there aren't, really—not when you're trying to collect them." She paused. "Also, you don't know exactly *why* a bird would lose a feather. I mean, it might be sick or something. Like there's a disease parrots get—"

"Wanda, didn't you ever hear of birds molting?" Steve interrupted. "Maybe I can't tell one bird from another, but even I know about that." It was his second interruption, he realized; he'd better get a grip on himself, if only for Motley's sake. One thing he'd learned about dog-training—you had to stay calm on the outside no matter what you were feeling inside.

"Anyway, I did save a couple of blue-jay feathers to stick in my hair," Wanda went on. "I soaked them in some of my dad's Listerine mouthwash, just in case. But then Mrs. Rowan gave me this. I think it comes from ostriches." From her tote bag she extracted a bizarre object that looked like nothing so much as the tail of some monstrous cat—a cat, moreover, that had been in a bad fight. Motley sat up and growled. "It's called a boa. You wear it around your neck."

"You got that from Mrs. Rowan?" Sally said incredulously.

"Yes, she said it was a present someone gave her a long time ago and she'd always hated it—well, she's a conservationist and everything—but somehow she never got around to throwing it away."

Everyone looked at Rita, who shrugged. "It sure doesn't look like anything she'd ever wear."

Fred said knowledgeably, "You see those a lot in old movies, the kind where people are always drinking champagne and going to nightclubs."

Motley was still growling. Steve told him to shut up, and asked Wanda if she'd mind putting the boa back in her bag for now. She obliged. A feathery black tip still protruded, twitching like a live thing. Only when she'd stuffed the tip out of sight and covered the top of the bag with her towel did Motley relax and lie back down again.

As the rehearsal got under way, Steve tried to block out everything but how well his charge was behaving. Motley didn't howl when Gus played "The Streets of Laredo," though Steve wouldn't have blamed him. Nor did he do anything worse than cower under the Ping-Pong table when one of Angie's makeshift taps flew off the bottom of her shoe and skidded across the floor. (She hadn't brought her tap shoes, after all, so had glued some flattened bottle caps to the soles of her Nikes.) He did bark a few times when Sally donned a pair of oversized dark glasses for her impersonation of Jackie O.; Steve had noticed he didn't like people to wear dark glasses. Still, even when Rita began twirling her lariat around, Motley only sat up and panted, following the loops of the rope with his muzzle.

"Hey, I got a great idea!" Fred exclaimed. He pounded a fist on one of his drums, producing a *brrong!* that made everyone jump. "How about roping the dog? I mean, as long as he's in the show anyway . . . a four-footed animal, see? It'd be more like the real thing." More than roping Karen, he meant.

Rita eyed Motley doubtfully. "I don't know. If he ran around too much, I might not be able to catch him. Anyway, wouldn't he mind?"

"Yes," said Steve, outraged. "He would mind. And so would I."

"Oh, come on," Angie urged, clapping her hands gleefully. "Let Rita try it, at least."

"Steve could always tell him to sit," Sally said mischievously. "Although I guess that would be cheating. I mean, you can't just tell a horse or a cow to sit when you want to rope it."

"A steer," Rita corrected her, and looked back at Motley. "I don't know," she said again. "I wouldn't want to scare him."

"Well, I do know," Steve said heatedly. "Motley is not a steer *or* a horse, just a poor mixed-up dog, and no one's gonna start slinging ropes around him." Actually he wasn't at all sure Motley would be scared by having a lariat flung at him—he was just as likely to think it was a game and try to catch it in his teeth. Either way, though, the result would be pandemonium; and besides, there was Motley's dignity to consider. And besides that—

"He's the Kirbys' dog, remember? You want to try

putting a noose around his neck, you better check it out with them first."

"Right," Gus said, when this seemed to settle the matter, and consulted the alarm clock he'd set on top of the piano as a timer. "Rita, you done for now?"

Rita looked offended. "I still have my circles and jumps, remember?"

While she was doing them, Wanda produced a pair of jay feathers from her tote bag and stuck them behind her ears. Since her ears were rather prominent anyway, Steve thought this made her look like some weird kind of insect, a moth maybe, with blue antennae. Then she dragged out the feather boa and draped it around her shoulders. "Does anyone have some rubber bands?" she asked, clutching at the floating, wispy ends. "I could make it look like wings, sort of, if I fastened the ends to my wrists. Or maybe my elbows."

With an air of mild bemusement, Motley had been watching Rita spin and stomp. Now he turned his head, just as Wanda gestured with one arm and the boa slithered sideways. If Steve hadn't been sitting on the edge of the Ping-Pong table, Motley's lunge would have dragged it halfway across the room. As it was, he stood straining at the end of the leash, barking and growling, the multicolored fur of his ruff standing on end.

"Motley, it's just *feathers*," Steve yelled into the din. "Here, look." He grabbed a stray black feather out of the air—talk about molting, the boa seemed to be in a terminal state of shedding—and held it in front of

Motley's nose. Motley ignored it, his gaze fixed on the writhing, snaky shape of the boa itself.

"Maybe if I showed it to him," Wanda said. Unfurling the boa, she took a step toward Motley, who backed away with a snarl that bared his teeth.

"Okay, that's it!" Gus exploded. "Get that dog out of here. Tie him up outside, pitch him in the lake, I don't care, but for Pete's sake, get that stupid mutt out of this rehearsal!"

"With pleasure." Steve bent to untie Motley's leash. "In fact, we'll *both* get out of here for good, all the way out of this pathetic show. Talk about stupid—Motley is positively brilliant compared to most of the people in this room. Come on, Motley. If they want to make fools out of themselves, that's their business."

The fury in his voice—maybe also the fact that Wanda had hurriedly crammed the boa back into her tote bag—arrested Motley in midgrowl. He sank onto his haunches and looked up at Steve anxiously. There was a sudden silence.

"So that's what you think," Gus said.

"Yes. And so do you." They exchanged glares. Gus was the first to look away.

"I knew it," Angie said dolefully, waving away an errant feather. Then she looked at the black fluff clinging to Wanda's white T-shirt and giggled. "I guess the show really is pretty terrible, isn't it? I don't mean just you, Wanda," she added.

"I know," Wanda said.

Fred cleared his throat. "Now, just a minute, guys.

Sure, things are still a little rough, but you know what they say about a bad dress rehearsal—"

"Oh, come *on*," Sally said. "Rough? It's a disaster." She exhaled loudly, as if this was something she'd been wanting to say for a long time.

Hugh said hopefully, "But we're having fun, though, right? I mean, we're not just gonna . . . well . . . quit, are we?"

No one answered him. Rita had been chewing thoughtfully on the tail of her braid; now she flipped it over the shoulder of her leather-fringed Western shirt—she was wearing a pair of mangy-looking chaps as well—and addressed Steve. "Okay, if you think it's so terrible, tell us how to fix it."

"Oh, no," Steve said, holding up a hand. "I'm not walking into that trap. For one thing, you already have a fixer, good old Fred here"—he shot an inimical glance at Fred, who smiled uncertainly—"and for another, I've had it with everyone saying that all I want to do is boss people around."

"Well, but just for instance," Rita persisted.

Steve hesitated, studying the circle of faces. Even Gus seemed to be gazing at him expectantly, if in a grudging sort of way. Only Fred continued to look bewildered.

"You're gonna be mad at some of the stuff I have to say," he warned.

"That's okay," Sally told him. The others nodded.

"Well, then . . ." Steve checked Motley's leash and told him to lie down. Then he leaned back against the Ping-Pong table and folded his arms. "What I think is, you're all trying to be too fancy. For instance, Wanda should just do her bird calls, not try to look like a bird, or for Pete's sake *act* like one." Wanda looked relieved. "If she wants to liven up her act a bit"—in passing, Steve was proud of the delicate way he'd put this—"she could have the audience try to guess the birds she's imitating."

"Good thought," Fred exclaimed, as if struck by the originality of this idea. "Hey, maybe she could show pictures too—that'd be really educational. Well, I guess pictures might be kind of hard to see, but if we could get hold of some slides of birds—"

"As for Rita," Steve went on, ignoring him, "she should settle for roping a chair, or maybe the piano, like Gus said. From what I've seen, it could take her four or five tries to land her rope around a person, and someone might get hurt, the way all the little kids will be sitting up front." Rita bit her lip but didn't protest. Gus was looking gratified, an expression that deepened as Steve continued. "And Gus should forget about those dumb hats—or rather the hats and the rifle. For Pete's sake, they didn't even *have* rifles back in that old-time war the song is about."

"Well, then, what about a sword?" Fred began, and stopped when everyone frowned at him.

"Angie, you should do one kind of dancing, not three," Steve told his sister ruthlessly. "Ballet, I guess, since you've already rigged up that cute little skirt." Forswearing the bathroom curtains, Angie had borrowed a spangled white chiffon scarf from her mother and basted it around the waist of her blue bathing suit. Since she hadn't allowed for the elastic quality of the suit, most of the stitches had already popped.

"Oh, come on, Steve, that's mean!" Angie looked around for support, but no one quite met her eyes.

"As for Hugh, he should do the four magic tricks that always work and skip the other four." Actually, Steve wasn't sure Hugh had even four tricks that wouldn't come unglued, so to speak, during the performance, but never mind; he hurried on to Sally. "And Sally should stop trying to act out celebrities, except maybe Princess Di, and do people around here instead. Like Doris— well, maybe not Doris," he amended on second thought, "but Ray, for instance, and Mrs. Rowan and Pierre."

Sally's face brightened. "How about Mr. Jeffries' nurse? I wouldn't do anything *nasty*," she assured them. "Just—well—" She shifted on her folding chair, squared her shoulders, and picked up an imaginary pair of knitting needles. Instantly you could see the nurse's heavy jowls and hear the rustle of starch as she crossed her linebacker's calves. Even Gus smiled.

"Now, about Fred—" Steve paused, reminding himself to choose his words carefully. "I think Fred should be first on the program, not last. You know, to start things off with a bang." And get all that racket over with, he added to himself. "Then Gus can come last, so the show ends real quietly and—you know—dramatically. 'Nobody Knows the Trouble I've Seen'. . . well, everyone has troubles, right? Leave 'em with something to think about."

There was a silence as everyone pondered this subtle artistic effect (not bad, Steve thought, considering it was right off the top of his head). After a visible struggle with himself, Fred said, "Well, at least that way I can have all my drums and stuff in place before the curtain opens."

"Opens how?" Steve looked pointedly at the laundry line of limp sheets, one of which he recognized now as the striped top sheet from his own bed—Angie was going to have a lot of bedmaking to do after the rehearsal. "With all those pulleys you were going to rig up?" Fred looked down at his drums. "Anyway, we don't need a curtain, we can just turn the room around."

When everyone gazed at him blankly, he gestured at the spacious rear of the rec house. "We need a back-stage, right?—somewhere we can keep our gear and put on our costumes, those that are wearing them, and make our entrances from. So we make that end of the room the stage, and just use the screen porch. Also, with all the windows there, we won't need any special lighting like good old Fred was going to fix up, especially if we do the show in the late afternoon, like Nora wants, instead of at night."

"Nora said it was okay to have it at night," Angie protested.

"She was being nice," Steve explained. "I mean, a bunch of kids putting on a show? Everyone will have to come—I don't mean they won't *want* to, but also they'll have to—and what with Saturday being buffet night, it'll be a lot easier for the staff if we do it before dinner."

He thought a moment. "And I guess that's all I have to

say, except I'd like to be near the beginning of the program instead of the end, so Motley won't get too restless."

This wasn't a problem at the moment—Motley was stretched out snoring under the Ping-Pong table, evidently exhausted by his encounter with the feather boa. At the sound of his name, he stirred, cocked the one ear that would cock, and went back to sleep. There was a buzz of conversation among the performers. Rita was in favor of starting the rehearsal over again and doing it Steve's way, and after some token protests, the others— except for Fred, frowning down at his drums—agreed. Even Angie said with a sigh, "Oh, well, I guess we should have let Steve be in charge all along. He's the only one who really knows how to do things *right*."

Steve looked apprehensively at Gus, who shrugged, stuck his hands in his pockets, and finally produced a sheepish grin.

Fred, however, had finally gotten mad. (Actually Steve rather envied Fred his long fuse, his own being so short; though he also thought it was probably one of the things that was wrong with him.) "Why didn't you say any of this stuff before?" he demanded, leaving the shelter of his drums to plant himself in front of Steve, his round chin thrust forward. "And if you're always so right about everything, why did you let my brother go off sailing without that board thing?"

Gus said hotly, "He did try to tell you about it, remember? But you were so sure your wonderful big brother knew all there was to know about sailing." The partisan scorn in his voice was music to Steve's ears.

"Well, okay"—Fred blinked defensively behind his smeary glasses—"but why didn't he tell *Todd*? Why didn't he just go outside and yell at him?"

"I was trying not to embarrass him," Steve said, and was conscious of several thoughtful glances turned on him.

"It sure didn't work out that way," Fred objected. "He was plenty embarrassed."

"Thanks to his idiot girlfriend," Steve said, finally allowing himself the luxury of losing his temper. "Though she's a good cut above your bonehead of a big brother—at least she knows enough to know what she doesn't know. People who don't know that much *deserve* to be embarrassed."

He was aware that this wasn't as clear as it might have been, also that he'd probably just blown it as far as the Erskines were concerned, but somehow he didn't care. He gazed out the window for a moment at the blue waters of Heron Lake, spattered with water lilies whose roots were nourished by the rich black mud of the bottom. Then he turned back to Fred, who was looking stunned. "So okay, maybe your family has a whole lot of money, and maybe Potter's can use it, but I say the heck with it. I'd rather have the place close down than see it paved over and dredged out and built up to be all bright and shiny and new looking, with boats zooming around on Great Harriman so your brothers can water-ski."

"Close down?" said Sally.

"What are you talking about?" Gus demanded.

124

But Fred was still staring at Steve. "What did you call my brother?"

"A bonehead," Steve repeated with relish. "As far as I can see, he's got muscles where his brains ought to be. And he's not exactly big on manners, either. He didn't even thank me after I rowed out to help him."

"He never says please, either," Hugh contributed unexpectedly. "When Andrew and I were playing badminton and he wanted to play, he just caught the bird after Andrew hit it and told us to get lost."

"Yeah, I'd sure hate to have *him* for an older brother," Angie said. "I mean, Steve can be pretty rude sometimes, but at least he's smart."

"Well, but brains—" Fred was frowning. "See, brains don't matter if you're big and strong and good-looking and can *do* stuff. That's why I'm the idea man in our family, sort of—because I can't. Do anything, I mean. I guess the genes ran out by the time they got to me," he explained sadly. "Like I'm the runt of the family, see? Though my dad thinks I might be a throwback to my great-grandfather on his side. He was an inventor."

While Steve was contemplating Fred in the role of inventor, Rita asked in her blunt way, "How do you *know* you can't do stuff? Do you ever try?"

"Oh, well—" Fred shrugged, then shook his head. "Not much," he confessed. "I tried baseball for a couple of days at school, but all I ever did was strike out. I have a permanent gym excuse, see, because of my adenoids."

No one wanted to explore the subject of Fred's adenoids.

"Maybe if you cleaned your glasses—" Angie ventured.

"And lost some weight," Sally put in. "I've been watching you eat—well, not really *watching* you," she qualified as Fred looked startled, "just noticing, the way our table is next to yours. And it's like you're trying to keep up with your brothers, only they have the build for it and you don't."

Even Wanda seemed to feel this was a less than tactful observation. She said kindly, "I saw you skipping stones over at Great Harriman the other day, down along the shore trail, and you were really good. One of them skipped six times. That's more than my father can do, even."

Fred looked pleased. "Yeah, well, skipping stones is sort of a hobby of mine. In fact, I've been thinking there oughtta be some way of packaging it as a game—you know, for people who don't live near the water. Like if you stretched a big piece of foil, or maybe plastic wrap—hey, yeah, maybe that blue kind—over a bamboo frame—"

"Why bamboo?" Steve found himself asking; then he said hastily, "Listen, if we're gonna start this rehearsal over, we better get going."

"Oh, right," Fred said, nodding agreeably.

Steve eyed him with an exasperation that verged on despair. Obviously it wasn't going to be possible to stay mad at Fred, as he'd been looking forward to doing, if Fred had already forgotten being mad at him. Resignedly he said, "Here, Fred, I'll give you a hand with those drums—we need to move 'em up front. The new front, I mean. The rest of you guys turn some chairs around so we can get used to that end being the stage. And Wanda, why don't you put that bag of yours outside before Motley wakes up again."

He wasn't too surprised to find himself moving the drums on his own, while Fred bustled around collecting his kazoo and tambourine and cowbell.

"You know how to row a boat?" Steve overheard Hugh asking Fred. "Because if you don't, I just learned this year, and I could probably teach you if you want."

Steve groaned aloud. Gus looked over at him and grinned. "You want rescues, you got 'em," he said.

Chapter 10

Except for Motley, the talent show went off without a hitch—that is, if you didn't count Rita's bringing down a floor lamp (the one next to the piano) and Hugh's pouring a whole glass of water into his hat, to the mystification of some of the spectators and the hilarity of the rest. Luckily this was the last of his four tricks, since the hat would never be the same again, even if Hugh could manage to unstick the false rim of the glass. He thought he must have gotten some glue on it by mistake.

"Motley did great at the dress rehearsal," Gus tried to console Steve the next day. "Everyone was really impressed by how much you'd trained him. Especially at the end, when you put the dog biscuit on his paws and told him to leave it and he did."

"Yeah, well, I should have stuck with that instead of fooling around with that dumb hoop," Steve said bitterly. He'd been the latest to discover that out of the chaff of ideas Fred tossed into the air, one or two had a nasty way of sticking to you, like those little tickseeds with the forked tails. Not that having Motley go through a hoop had been an idea exactly, Steve acknowledged fairly; the hoops had been no more than a passing reference.

"Actually, it might have been okay if it hadn't been for the paper," he brooded. The paper he'd wrapped around the bike tire, he meant, colored orange by Angie and cut into little peaks to look like flames. "Motley went through the tire fine when we were practicing—not *jumping,* I mean, there wasn't time to teach him that, but just walking through it in, you know, a casual kind of way. But then in the show . . . I think it was mostly the way the paper crackled."

"Something sure spooked him," Gus agreed.

Steve winced, trying to shut out the picture of Motley seizing the hoop in his jaws and shaking it back and forth, then racing wildly around the rec house until finally he was collared by Mr. Jeffries' nurse, stationed in her usual post by the door.

"Also, I should have told the Kirbys to sit in back. It didn't help any, the way they started in clapping and cheering."

Steve had made what he still considered an impressive entrance, at least to anyone who knew Motley. He'd come in from the screened porch with Motley at his heel—no leash or anything—and walked slowly around the stage area several times, with Motley still heeling closely, like a dog-show dog. Then he'd told Motley to sit, which he did instantly. At this point Mrs. Kirby rose from her chair and applauded. When Motley was ordered to lie down and did that too, Mr. Kirby also stood up. "Way to go, Motley!" he yelled.

And that, in retrospect, was pretty much that. Once it dawned on Motley that his owners were actually in the room, right there among all those other people, he never really got his concentration back. Nothing Steve could say would induce him to roll over like they'd practiced, let alone play dead; and when Steve told him "Stay!" he wandered back onto the screened porch and had to be shooed back onstage with loud hisses by the other performers.

The two boys were silent for several minutes, sitting side by side on a log where they'd stopped to rest during their circuit of the Ledge Trail. A bird called from somewhere in the dense canopy of leaves that was just beginning to patter with rain. Steve thought he recognized it as a phoebe from one of Wanda's whistles. This made him feel better for some peculiar reason—he didn't really see the point of cluttering up your mind with a lot of names when you were just trying to relax outdoors. What really cheered him, though, was the realization that he and Gus were friends again somehow, back to the way they'd been before, and without even needing to talk about it.

"Oh, well," Steve said at last, "if anyone had to foul up, I'm just as glad it was me." When Gus looked puzzled, he explained. "See, if I'd turned out to be the star of the show, everyone would have said I was showing off. This way, no one can say that."

"No," Gus agreed. After a pause, he said reflectively, "I guess if there was a star, it was Sally. She was really funny doing those impersonations—not just the ones she did in rehearsal, I mean, but the other ones people called out for her to do. Like Terence trying to flip pancakes in the morning while he's still half-asleep."

Steve had to take this on faith, since he'd been in the process of dragging Motley back to the Kirbys' cabin at the time and had missed the whole of Sally's act—including her impression of Mr. Jeffries' nurse, which was something he'd been looking forward to especially.

Gus had lapsed into silence again, smoothing the leaves of a fern he'd plucked from beside the trail. "You ever go dirt-biking?" he asked.

"No. It looks like fun, though. Why?"

"That Fred. He's talking about getting a dirt bike and bringing it up here next year."

"Dirt-biking *here?*" Steve was aghast. He looked around at the quiet, dusky shapes of the trees, at the soft carpet of leaves and needles and moss. "He can't! Have you ever seen what those bikes do to a place? I don't think the grass even grows back where they've been, never mind plants and bushes and things. And the noise—well, you can forget about the deer and raccoons and possums and chipmunks, and probably the birds too."

"Of course, Fred talks about a lot of stuff he never does," Gus pointed out. "But this sounded like he might really mean it. And if the Erskines are gonna put a lot of money into Potter's, like you said they might . . ." He shrugged morosely.

The Erskines were leaving the next day, but had signed up for two weeks the next summer, maybe three if Mr. Erskine didn't have any business emergencies like mergers or stock splits or hostile takeovers.

Steve got to his feet, still agitated. "Listen, I bet they don't even *allow* dirt bikes here. Maybe there's a state law or something, like the one they're always trying to pass against snowmobiles in the winter. Come on, let's go find Nora and ask her. I've gotta go back anyway because of the tennis tournament—I told my parents I'd watch the finals."

"It's raining," Gus observed.

"Yeah, but not very hard, and the Curtises are leaving in the morning, so they have to get it done today." Steve's mood lightened a little. "Boy, just think how *calm* it's gonna be around here without Fred and Hugh." He turned onto the trail. "You coming? The tennis might be pretty good, actually. Mr. and Mrs. Kirby had a fight this morning over whether they should hire a dog-walker for Motley when they get home—Mr. Kirby didn't want to spend the money and said he'd do it himself and Mrs. Kirby said, like when, in the middle of the night?—so they'll really be gunning for each other."

Gus hunched his shoulders, gazing down through the woods at the distant silvery glint of Great Harriman. "It's good fishing weather. Maybe I'll go down on the shore trail for a while, see what's happening."

"What could be happening? A lake being rained on, that's all," Steve said impatiently. "Anyway, you don't have your rod."

"I know. But sometimes if you just mosey around for a while, you can sort of get an idea how the fish might be feeling—you know, the mood they're in, and how they're likely to act."

Steve shook his head, deciding he would never fathom the part of Gus's mind that was involved with fish, and strode back to camp on his own. He didn't have far to look for Nora, or for Ray either. They were on the kitchen porch, polishing up a large brass cuspidor that had been part of the lodge's original furnishings and now served as the trophy for the tennis tournament.

"Have a rag," Ray said as Steve joined them, tossing him a scrap of flannel. "We always forget about this darn thing until the last minute."

"Yes, I don't know why we don't switch to something easier," Nora said. "A Styrofoam ice bucket, for instance. Of course, you can't engrave Styrofoam." She looked at Steve. "Something on your mind?"

"It's about dirt-biking," Steve said, reaching for the can of Brasso. He'd planned to present his objections to this activity calmly and rationally; but somehow, as he rubbed away unseeingly at the tarnished brass, he found he wasn't just talking about dirt-biking but about all the horrific changes he foresaw overtaking Potter's if the Erskines had their way. "It'll wind up turning into a *resort*," he finished bitterly.

"Steve, hold on a minute!" Nora took the rag out of

his hand. "You're wearing a hole in the side. Now, listen to me: the Erskines love Potter's just the way it is. Mr. Erskine said it's the first time he's really relaxed since he made all his money and started getting carried away. He said he'd forgotten how comfortable it was just to be simple and shabby. As for investing in the corporation— well, we did hint at the possibility, very delicately, but he said it was early days, and in any case he'd have to put his lawyers on it. Somehow I can't see the lawyers recommending Potter's as an addition to his portfolio," she finished wryly.

"Anyway, he's certainly not going to let anyone bring a dirt bike up here," Ray assured Steve, "no matter what Fred says. Fred does tend to run off at the mouth a bit, you know," he added, in what Steve considered the understatement of the year. Ray gave a last swipe to the cuspidor and stood up. "Okay, that's good enough. Help me load this thing onto the wheelbarrow, will you, Steve, and we'll take it over to the court."

"Well, but—" Steve grasped one of the handles and almost staggered under the unexpected weight—the thing must be lined with lead. "What about the repairs, then . . . all the stuff that needs doing? Will there be enough money to fix the roof?"

"The roof?" Nora followed Steve's upward gaze at the steeply pitched eaves of the lodge, at the cedar shingles splotched with damp, at the massive chimneys standing square against the pearly, cloud-dappled sky. "Oh, Steve, it's the *car shed* roof that needs fixing—just those old sheets of tin that are rusting out. Not that tin is cheap these days, but we'll manage somehow—we always do."

"Good, the rain seems to be letting up," Ray observed as they trundled the wheelbarrow around the corner of the veranda. "Still, just as well the court's as much sand as clay these days."

Steve heard the pleasant, summery, idle-sounding plonk of tennis balls and saw that the players had begun to warm up. Wanda was wearing a big yellow rain hat and had covered the handle of her racket with foil, presumably to keep it dry. He grinned. "I'm surprised Wanda doesn't have spikes on her tennis shoes."

Ray grinned back before he caught himself; as a good host, he made it a principle never to indulge in flippancy where his guests were concerned. "Sounding more like your old self, Steve," he grunted as they hefted the cuspidor onto the trestle table. "You were keeping such a low profile there for a while, we hardly recognized you. Not really your style, I'd say."

"No," Steve agreed, though he felt gratified that someone had noticed. "Hey, you want me to referee?" he asked, looking at the tall stepladder that had been set up beside the court as a referee stand.

"No thanks, I'll handle it myself," Ray told him.

"I could spell you—" he began, but Ray gave him a look. "Better not, Steve," he warned.

Steve thought for a moment, then nodded. As he took a seat on the sidelines, though, he couldn't help making a bet with himself that Ray would be sorry, especially if the match turned out to be a long one; like a lot of other things at Potter's, that stepladder had seen better days. He also congratulated himself on the fact that he'd never said anything to Gus about the lodge roof. If there was one thing Steve really hated, it was being wrong.